EVE IMMACULATE

EVE IMMACULATE

Robin Fox

Printed in the United States of America

ISBN 979-8-3604-1398-1

Contents

For my mom, the ultimate storyteller,
for bringing forth the creative gene that
begs us to make art, no matter what.

CHAPTER 1

Grace

I was sleeping under my grandmother's quilt the night the Black River ate Grace Adams alive. It pulled her in, opened her blue lips, and filled her innocent body while I was in my bed surrounded by my open books. Maybe it was God that poured the river down her pale throat, along with one black pebble that settled in her belly, and left her earth form bloated, floating. She was returned to the earth just as she came, in dark water. Mrs. Adams says that because God took her so young, she is forever an angel. And I am trying to believe her. I could really use an angel.

Grace was wearing her seat belt. That was what kept her tethered to the sinking car. Patrick, her brother, had seen that news story on sinking cars. He remembered the thing about the seat belt, that getting it off was the first thing to do, and he went into action. He rolled down his window and yelled to his sister. But she had hit her head and was confused. He pushed his mother across him and out the window where the water rushed in, but she wouldn't swim out. So he stayed with her and got her to the surface. He couldn't see the bank, but he pushed until she had her head up. When he dove back for Grace, the car was gone. It was total blackness. I read all of this in the newspaper, and Mrs. Adams told me some details when she was ready to talk. The story of the sixteen-year- old boy trying to save his baby sister was big news. It was a miracle Patrick and his mother made it out alive.

Grace was my best friend. We were in the Bend Hill High School Orchestra together. She played the viola and I, the cello. Grace wore a cross around her neck that she did not take off for anything. I thought that protected her from the dangers in the world. I was wrong. God wanted her home, her mother told me. She was just too good for this world. So, she is an angel now, and that way she is with us every day, and she gets the good life. I am supposed to feel God to feel her near me. That night God was the river. Today He might be the moon. I was working hard to feel God so I could feel Grace again, but it was harder than you think to feel something no one has ever seen or proven to be real. When you are born into that story, and it is reinforced every Sunday, at least, it comes naturally. But my family just gets bagels on Sunday and reads the *New York Times*. Now I need more than what is in front of me. I need to know she is okay.

If Grace is with God, she would want me to find them. I thought I might be getting close. I had started to slip out of my bed late at night and into hers, through her bedroom window. Maybe He was guiding me there. I could climb into her bed for a few hours before dawn, and no one even knew. Although it's possible they did know, and just left me alone.

Her window was always unlocked. My parents were freaking out. They wanted me to stop visiting Mrs. Adams so much, and they wanted me to talk about my new obsession with the Bible. "It's important literature. I'm just reading," I said. "Don't you want me to read?" They made me go to a psychiatrist, Dr. Julia Phillips, once a week. I told her I was just interested in religion, and Mrs. Adams was my Christian source. "What about Buddhism and Hinduism," she asked me. "Do you have a Buddhist source?" She had me there.

I felt connected to Grace when I read the stories she loved. Christmas was coming and I wanted to feel for the first time the real meaning of the holiday that I associated with lights and waking at dawn to see what Santa had brought for me. Before, I just thought about the ornaments and the presents. Now, I wanted to know what Mary was thinking. She was a teenage girl like us. Grace had a picture of Mary the size of a postcard in her room right beside her bed. It was a real oil painting from a street artist that her aunt brought her from Rome. That picture always fascinated me. In it, Mary's eyes tilted up and slightly to the left. The angel Gabriel was above her with his halo, real small like a fairy. Grace could not believe that my family did not believe in Jesus.

"I don't think they don't believe in him. They just don't think about Jesus at all, and they don't buy that he is the son of God, and the rising from the dead part. That's for sure."

"But what DO they believe?"

"My mom says she believes in the goodness of people and

the beauty of this world, all connected by a powerful energy, and the idea that collectively we are a force."

"That is not really a belief. It sounds like more of a hope."

"My dad believes there is a God. But, you know, he just doesn't go to church or temple or whatever. He says God is inside us."

"What about Heaven? What about when you die?"

"I don't think they believe in Heaven, really, even though they said Martha went to Heaven when she died." Martha was our dog. She died when I was eight.

"What will happen to them . . . or you, then?"

"Nothing. Just nothingness. You're just gone, returned to the earth. It's a circle, you replenish the soil."

"Ew. That is so sad, Eve. And scary. Dirt, they think you become dirt? What do you believe?" Grace asked, pleading with her eyes.

"I guess I believe there might be a Heaven," I answered cautiously.

"Eve, you have to accept Jesus as your savior to go to Heaven. You have to."

"Okay, I'm trying. I just can't be sure."

"I pray for you every night," Grace sighed.

"Good. Then I know I will get in."

This is why Grace died in the accident, while my mom would not let me go to the play that night. See, the way I see it, Grace saved my life because God knew that I would have burned in Hell, but Gracie exists now in a golden, forest-filled world with rainbows every day and baby animals under all the bushes. I owe my life to her so I need to try to believe in her God. But I'd rather be dead than be here without her.

I go to school and sit in the back. I listen most of the time. I do my work. My grades have not suffered much. It is not so hard to keep up at Bend Hill, especially when you have no social life. Grace and I were just our own team of weirdos. We didn't fit into high school life so much, so we hung with each other. I don't have a group, like the theater kids or the basketball team. I am in the orchestra, but we don't make a group like the band does. It was just me and my cello, and Grace and her viola, and Sara Herrington, the other cellist who sits next to me, and a bunch of kids I never talk to. I talk to Sara occasionally. But she only plays because her mom makes her. She doesn't feel the music. She'd rather be in dance. Only Grace and I played outside of school. We did duets, her playing the violin part. We performed for our parents, and we both made All-State. I'm not cute, or beautiful, so I don't belong to the popular crowd either. My hair is too curly, and I don't like makeup. I am certainly not athletic in the team sport way, even though I run. And I am not even a science geek or the brainy type. I make good grades, and I speak French pretty well because my parents made us move to Paris for a year when my sister, Raine, was in middle school and hanging with a bad crowd. I was nine, and I didn't know Grace then. The Adamses moved to Bend Hill when I was ten. Since then, we have been inseparable according to our parents, though that is an exaggeration. We met when my mom made me take over some lemon pound cake and her mother invited me in. I helped Grace unpack her things and we just clicked. I could tell she was like me, kind of shy and a big reader. She convinced me to start *The Chronicles of Narnia.* We became besties fast. She was like no one I had ever known, totally sure of herself. I always doubted myself, so I liked that. Even though my family was considered heathen, Mrs. Adams saw hope in me, so she let us be friends. She included me in all the family and holiday stuff. My family is pretty much wrapped up in newspapers, politics, books, local theater, and running. My parents are worldly and healthy and concerned with peace and civil rights. My dad is a lawyer, and my mom has her law degree, but she mostly volunteers as a child advocate now. Raine is five years older than me, and she finally settled down and went to college. My parents let her travel around Europe for a year first, as long as she was accepted into a school. We are very different and with the big gap in age, we are not so close. I am the one who flies low under the radar. But since Grace died, they are paying attention — too much, in my opinion. I have a right to be religious if I want. I can believe in Jesus. You'd think I was worshipping heroin. But I'm just looking for Grace, or at least some peace.

They gave me medication right after the funeral because I would not get out of bed, or talk. It helped me get through the days. Now I can just drift through things, and I spend my time reading. When I feel lonely, I visit Mrs. Adams. She is my new friend, I guess. Mrs. Adams is the kind of mom that looks like she would be really cool. First off, she is younger than most of the other mothers. She got married at twenty. Grace looked just like her. She is really pretty, with long dark hair and she wears these kind of hippie-like dresses, bohemian sort of. She is very voluptuous but natural, like a cross between Kim Kardashian and that actress in *Love Story*, which I watched with Mom recently. The guys call her a MILF, but actually, they are all scared of her because of the church thing. Weirdly, we are able to comfort each other.

Patrick can't stand to talk about Grace to his mom. He can't even look at her. He is on the lacrosse team, and he can get lost in that and school. He was going to be a rower, but since the accident, he cannot stand to be near water. I wonder if he saw her in there. I wonder if he sleeps. He is never home anymore. He is not like Gracie and me at all. He is the Prom King, or he was before he changed. When I come over, Mrs. Adams makes tea for us, or she lets me help her bake. She takes Bible study classes, and she tells me what she learns. She talks and I listen. I follow along with her class on my own. I mostly want to know about Mary. Sometimes I dream about the angel Gabriel. I try to imagine Grace with wings and her long hair down. She always had her hair in a ponytail, and I can't imagine an angel with a ponytail.

When I go to bed and turn out the lights, I lie so still. This is the time I think she will be in my room. Then I usually fall asleep, and I wake up around 2:30 in the morning. Every night I wake up between 2:28 and 2:34, and I think it must be Grace waking me. So that's when I started going downstairs and out the kitchen door and down the street four houses, and into the Adams' backyard, where I raise the window very quietly and climb in. Thank God they have a one-story house. It is called a split plan. Grace and Patrick have rooms on the east side, connected by a bathroom; their parents are on the other side of the house. I lie in her bed— it is the only good sleep I get—then I wake up around 5:30 and climb out the window and go back home. I am always falling asleep in class. My mother wants to adjust my medication or get me off of it by going to more therapy. Dr. Phillips is nice and all, but she doesn't change things. My best friend is dead. I don't have other best friends or a boyfriend. School is school. I can't talk about books and music and why there aren't any decent boys with my only friend anymore. What is there to get up for?

(PATRICK)

I wish I was the one who died. Instead, I have to fight through every day, my heart pounding, or drug myself, to escape the nights where I am alone with that river. There is only before, and after. I was one person before the accident, and now I am another. I was happy. I was lucky. I had friends and girls and focus. I was good at lacrosse and soccer without even trying. My parents thought I was a good son even though I was never as good as Grace. I did what I was asked. Except for their silly rules, everything was pretty easy, and I slept like a baby. I ate pizza on the weekends and pot roast on Wednesdays, I took out the garbage and I watched YouTube videos on my phone when I had done all the things they required. I was so fucking normal. I wish I had known what I had.

Then everything changed when we flew off the road in the dark and into that black hole. I lived to tell, and my little sister did not. I got out. I opened the window, and I pulled out my mom, and here we are. Grace did not follow us, and when I went back for her, the car and my baby sister were gone. I kept diving and surfacing until I could only kick the roof of the truck with my feet. On the last dive, I reached the glass and banged, but I couldn't find the open window. Where was she? I could only grasp at the heavy metal doors as the car settled downward. I could not hold my breath long enough to pry the door open. I had to believe she was out by then. "Please God, please God, please, please let Gracie be out." But when I screamed from the surface, there was no answer. By the time help came and found her, she was still strapped in her seat, her fingers pressed against the glass. They had to pull me out of the water. Since then, I do not sleep. I eat, but it never tastes like anything. I play ball and run to stay out of the house and keep moving, but it is not easy, or normal. I would rather be with Grace, or wherever she is, while she should be here. I want to take her place. She would take care of my mother. But I cannot do that. The sight of my mother makes my skin crawl now. I make my skin crawl. We are the same—survivors.

When I was four and Grace was three, we both went to the Methodist church preschool. It was really small and there was just a big room with the three-year-olds on one side and the four-year-olds on the other. There was some kind of partition, but we were all together some of the time. Grace insisted on being in my class in the chair next to me. At first, they led her away, and they spoke to our mom about separating us. But gradually Grace stayed longer and longer, and when they saw she could do all the letters and numbers that the four-year-olds did, they gave up and let her stay. That is probably why she was always better in school than me. I hugged her every so often and sucked on the end of her braid when I was bored or fidgety. She was my twin—Irish twins they called us, not even twelve months apart. We went to the school in the mornings and then we went home and played: Legos, house, school, forts under the dining room table, hide and seek, all the dumb games. She always chattered while I moved. She climbed on my back and rode me around the playroom. We shared a room and often ended up in the same bed. We were *both afraid of monsters. We giggled all the time. Then came kindergarten. I had to go to real school, and Grace had to stay in preschool. She refused to go the first week because I was not going to be there. She said she already did the Fours anyway. She wasn't wrong. But eventually she got bored at home, and she went to preschool, and I came home and told her all about kindergarten where we got to eat lunch in the cafeteria. We were best friends then. Our parents kept us wrapped up in church and Bible study and family dinners and chores, so we did not need anyone else.*

Until middle school. Again, I left her. I went to the new school while she stayed with the babies. I learned that girls thought I was good-looking and good at sports, and I liked that. All Grace ever cared about was Jesus, and she started to drive me crazy. She had perfect handwriting and read her Bible and brushed her ridiculously long hair. She got her own room and played dumb music and crocheted. She also had a new best friend, Eve, and they were always together whispering and playing their instruments. When she came to middle school, I pretended I did not know her. After a month there, everyone knew she was a Jesus freak, and I was embarrassed by her. I nodded to her if I saw her in the halls, but nothing else. She was pretty, though, so people didn't really bully her. It's a good thing because I don't know if I would have protected her.

On the night of the accident, we were all cranky. I could not believe my mom made me go to that stupid play on a school night in the cold rain. But anything with church took precedence. Even Grace was pissy because she was supposed to be studying for a big test. When it was over, we ran to the car and she yelled "shotgun," but I beat her there.

"I called shotgun," she squealed.

"So. You were too slow."

"Get in the car and stop yelling. I have a pounding headache," Mom said.

"I'll drive," I said.

"No. Not in this weather."

"But you have a migraine."

"I'll make it home."

Grace slammed her door and my mother yelled again. "Stop fighting!" I looked at her in the rearview mirror and smirked. That was the last time I saw her face. We swerved and spun and hit the cold water. I got my mom out somehow, and then I went back, and the car had disappeared. I dove and dove and could not find her. She drowned while I was screaming her name.

Now it is after. I am just here getting through the days. The days never seem to end. I lie in my bed awake, and I hear her little voice and I remember the taste of her braids in my mouth. She was perfect. She never did anything bad. She worshipped me. She wanted to be next to me always. And I left her over and over, and this time it's forever.

CHAPTER 2

Heaven

N obody knows that I tried to kill myself about a month after the funeral. I was just so lonely and miserable. In the beginning, they would not leave me alone. Then I took the medication and was able to go to school and sleep at night and all, and I started therapy, so my parents finally let me close the door to my room. I took a whole bottle of Excedrin. I guess I took too much because I threw it all up. I never told anyone, not even Dr. Phillips. I figured God did not want me. I would not get to be an angel.

That is when I got the Bible and began to read. I like that it starts with Eve. It feels like a sign. Not sure of what exactly. Eve was the first woman, even though she was responsible for the downfall of man. Gross. The Bible is sexist for sure. But me being Eve, I take it as proof that I am included. It feels nice to be a part of something. I still have time to redeem myself. Grace always said I just have to believe and pray. I know it's hard to believe, but I love the idea of resurrection. Christianity has a virgin birth and rising from the dead. These are two things that I always thought were just plain crazy. Only uneducated, simple people could believe them.

But now I am trying to see what they see, since there are a lot of Harvard-educated Christians. Christian doctors and government leaders. Like I say to Mom, the Obamas are Christian. I thought I must be named Eve for a reason. I asked my parents why they named me Eve, and my mother said that after Raine, which is a family name, but is simple and of nature, they wanted a name with the same qualities for me. They chose Eve and were sure it was the right name when I was born at 6:14 in the evening. Most babies are born in the morning apparently.

"What if I had been a boy?" I asked, thinking maybe Adam.

"We were thinking about River."

"Oh," I said. My parents are real earthy folks. Thank God I wasn't born a boy. Again, God took that into His own hands.

I asked my dad why he believes in God. He said that he was brought up to believe that there was more to life than what we see.

"Just look around. Sunrise. The sky. Each person uniquely different. Spring flowers. A new baby. It is clear to me that there is something bigger than what's in front of us."

"What about Mom?"

"She explains things with science and nature, and that is her choice. But I feel it. I feel there is more."

"Do you think he is a man with a beard and white hair?"

"No. I think God is energy, a force, like the best of us, or the best of all of us together. Kind of like light or sound. When I see a sunset, I think of God."

"Is that what Jews think?"

"Not really. But that is what I think."

"Are you Jewish even though you don't go to services or observe the holidays?"

"Yes, I consider myself a Jew. My parents are Jewish, and I have inside of me what I was taught about my heritage. It is more than religion. It is my culture, my family, the fact that we are the minority and were persecuted. That is in me, even though I do not practice, like the fact that I am male and good at math. I do not need to have a Seder to feel that."

"Did you want us to be Jewish?"

"I have always given you the stories of our culture. And you have Grandy and Grander to share the holidays with. I believe that you can decide for yourself when you are grown. I hope that you will choose to honor Judaism in your own way."

"What if I choose another religion?"

"You have that right. I hope that you will allow me to tell your children our history, though."

"Do you think you can be a religion that pulls from many religions?"

"Of course. Believing is just that, and if it is believing in good, regardless of the organization, it is all good."

"Grace says that you have to be saved by Jesus Christ in order to go to Heaven. That means no Jews in Heaven, or dogs, or Buddhists or Mom."

"She has the right to believe that, but I do not think that is the kind of Heaven we would want to go to."

"I want there to be a Heaven. And I want to go there so I can see her. Maybe she is wrong about who is there."

"Do you think a good God would only let one little part of the universe in, including all the rapists and murderers who are saved in the final hours, but not Mom or Martha?"

"No."

"Do you believe there is Heaven?" he asked me.

"I want to believe that we meet again somewhere."

"But you are not sure?"

"There is very little that I am sure about."

I asked Grace how a serial killer could go to Heaven and my family could not. She wrinkled her brow. She had not thought about this a lot.

"Because the killer can be forgiven. God is all about forgiveness. And your family can still be saved. I know you will be saved in the end, Evie. See, you have a choice about Heaven. God will wait for you to believe."

"It doesn't seem fair that that is the only criteria. What about living a good life?"

This is what we talked about before Grace died. I was the devil's advocate. But now I am starting to get it. Forgiveness may be the root of everything. I am working on forgiving. Forgiving God, Mrs. Adams who was driving the car, my mother who would not let me go to the play on a school night, even Grace, who didn't unbuckle her seat belt and went without me. And most of all, me. She asked me to go with them, but I said no, I had to study for the biology test. I would have been in the back seat with her, and I am sure I would have unbuckled us both. I should have been there. All this forgiving is a lot. It takes up all my time. Between that and understanding Jesus and Mary, I am exhausted.

Last year, I had a crush on a boy in orchestra. Jake Lowe. He plays the bass. He has longish hair and is really quiet. But I was too shy to talk to him, and he never noticed me, even though I sat right in front of him, and I walked next to him every morning before I set up. He smiled at me once. I could think of nothing else. It was a reason for me to go to school and find him in the halls. After a while, I saw him talking to Maggie Aames who plays the violin. I wasn't surprised. Boys never look at me. I have real curly hair and I have never worn mascara or lipstick. The straight-haired girls get the boys. Grace had straight black hair that had never been cut. She wore it in a ponytail that she could sit on. Boys looked at her. But she let it be known that she wasn't interested. "Boys are just trouble," she said. "I am waiting for a long time. For my soul mate." That feeling I had about Jake is how I am starting to feel about Jesus. I am all tingly inside, and I cannot wait to get to my Bible when I get home from school. I have been given a reason to live. It's not like I want to be Grace, but I want her to be proud of me. I want to keep her alive, I guess. She lived for her faith and when I read the Bible, I feel her approval and her excitement. I do not want to disappoint my dad, but I feel God coming through me in this way, and I have to honor that for Grace. I think he will understand. After all, Jesus was a Jew.

I really dread going to Dr. Phillips. It is useless, and it is a
waste of my time, now that I have something I want to do:
read. I have tried to keep my thoughts about Mary and Jesus
to myself, but Dr. Phillips is really good at getting me to say
things I had no intention of revealing. She says she is
interested in my knowledge of the Bible and wants to talk
about it. I think she really wants to find out if I know too
much, you know, like an obsession. Adults always want you
to be balanced, not too much or too little of anything. She
needs to report back to my parents that I should be
developing other interests. For that reason, I still take cello
lessons, and practice, and run with my mother every other
day, as much as I'd rather read in my bed. And I keep up
with homework. But now they are on me about my lack of
friends. As if I could go out and select a new best friend,
'cause they are a dime a dozen, and just get back in the
groove. And Mrs. Adams is my friend anyway.

But I have been getting nervous about my visits to
Grace's room in the middle of the night. I know it is a matter
of time before they find out, but I just can't stop. I feel at
peace only then. I feel the closest to Grace there. If I could
just ask if I could have permission to sleep there until this is
over, this grief? I could say that I need to sleep in her room
for a while because it helps me, and maybe no one would
even care. But maybe my parents would stop my contact with
Mrs. Adams altogether. And that is why I continue to sneak

in. I feel I should tell Mrs. Adams. But then again, I can't be sure of how she will react. Maybe she wants Grace's bed to remain untouched. Her scent is there, and now mine. I use the Dove soap that she always swore by, so that the scent is the same. But there was something about Grace's hair, so black and silty, she smelled of river even before, while I smell of sun. There is something softer and comforting about her bed. It's soothing. My bed is dry and crisp. I cannot sleep in it.

I began by asking Mrs. Adams if I could read in Grace's room. I miss her room, I said. We used to do our homework there and lie on the floor with magazines.

"Would it bother you if I read in her room?"

There was a little flicker on her face of shock, maybe even anger, but she corrected herself and made her face soft again.

"You are welcome to spend time in Gracie's room anytime, Eve. Are you sure it's not too sad, too still? I go in there and I just can't stay because it is so still. I can feel Grace in the kitchen, but her room makes me sad."

"I think I feel her in her room. I spent so much time there, and now I . . . I . . . her room is all I have of her."

"Then you should be there. We haven't changed it. The sheets are still on the bed. Her homework is on the desk." I knew this, of course.

"Would you mind if I read her Bible?"

"Oh Eve, she would love that."

She put her hands on my shoulders, like they do in TV shows, old ones, and she said, "I am so lucky that you visit me and talk to me about Grace. The cake needs 25 minutes, why don't you go on to her room. You know where she keeps the Bible."

"Thanks, Mrs. Adams."

I used to envy Grace. She was very beautiful in a simple way. She was dramatic looking with her black hair and pale, pale skin, while I feel so ordinary. I hate my hair. It is too curly and tangled usually, while Grace's hair made you think of a waterfall and geishas and volcanoes. People made fun of the fact that she never cut it. They called her a Jesus freak. She ignored them and swished it behind her.

"Why don't you ever cut your hair?" I asked.

"It is my gift. It is my best feature."

"It would be healthier if you trimmed the ends, though."

"When I was little, I read a story about a girl whose hair touched the ground. I wanted to be her."

"Sounds like a lot of work to me."

"Well, now I know it is kind of silly, but I am afraid to break the tradition."

"I'll trim it for you, just the ends. You can trust me."

"Maybe."

She let me cut it in her bathroom. The last six inches were damaged, and I wanted to take it to where it was silky and shiny, but I stopped at two inches so she would trust me. It looked better, even though no one noticed but us, and her mother. She kept the hair in an envelope in the Bible. When I opened it, the envelope fell out, and I reached in and touched her hair. I read in the rocker until I heard the buzzer in the kitchen. Then I put the envelope in my pocket and left the room.

We make cakes every Friday afternoon now. I took one home for my family for the weekend. We are not a baking family. We are a brown rice and order-in Thai food family. My mother asked me how I thought Mrs. Adams was doing.

"You know, she seems okay," I said. "Or at least for someone whose daughter is dead."

"But I wonder how she gets out of bed each day. I could not go on," my mom sighed.

"You'd have to. You'd have Dad and Raine."

"But she was driving. I don't think I could bear it, knowing I was the driver. I just don't. I feel real pain for her."

"Mom," I said, "she has faith. She believes God took Grace for a reason, and she will see her again. That's how she gets out of bed."

My mother turned to me and locked eyes. "That is why religion exists. For situations like this."

"You mean it's just a crutch."

"Yes."

"How do you know?"

"I don't. But Evie, do you really believe that God took Grace, and that Mrs. Adams doesn't feel a little responsible? Even if it was an accident. Is her God someone who would do that to a mother and to you, her best friend? If so, how can she worship that God?"

"If there is a bigger plan, maybe. She gets to be with God.

We have to bear . . . yes, bad things happen to good people. Maybe Grace got the better deal . . . being in Heaven so young. Mrs. Adams sees her there living the life."

"Eve, that sounds very cult-like. Remember that the Adamses were raised in a closed society practically. They got married when they were children. They have never even been out of the country. There is nothing wrong with that, but you have to understand that they have a very small circle of influence, so God and Heaven are all they know. I am glad you find comfort in God. I just want you to remember that we humans are responsible for most of what happens in our lives. And then there are accidents, things we just cannot control."

"If I died, do you think you might consider God and Heaven?"

"I hope something would give me peace."

"What else is there?" I asked.

"My family," she said.

"But your family would be altered. You would need something that doesn't change. You would need a rock."

"If you died, Eve, I would need you. Nothing would change that."

This is supposed to make me feel better?

CHAPTER 3

Running

W hen I play the cello alone, I play the slow, sad songs. I feel the music coming through my bones more than I hear it. When Grace and I played duets, I listened with my ears. But now it is like running. It is physical. There is the bow with its hair and the instrument, and my bony knees, and my heart beating and the vibration that drowns the beating. When I run, I feel the same vibration and beat and breath. I can run forever now. At first, I did it to please my parents. I did it with dread, even though I felt wonderful afterward. Now I look forward to the pounding. My mother is aware of the change. I tell her I have the time now that I don't have my friend. Of course, I am a better runner. She wants me to run long distance on the team. I roll my eyes. Isn't it enough that I run with her? When will it ever be enough?

"Evie, I don't care about the team. I just want you to meet some new people who you might have something in common with. It's not like you have to find your soul mate, but there might be someone who is just kind or interesting. Loneliness is a silent illness." She is always reading stuff like this.

"I am never lonely," I say.

"Okay, but that's just it. You should feel lonely when you have no one to talk to. You're a teenage girl and everyone needs some level of companionship."

"I'm not like other teenage girls. I like to be alone. I prefer books."

"So, tell me, what are you reading?"

I hesitate. "*Ordinary People*," I mumble.

"Really? I remember reading it in high school. What do you think?"

"I think he is like me." Her eyes widen.

"I'm not going to kill myself. I just mean because he is the one left."

"And he is so unhappy he doesn't want to live," she says.

I see my poor mother's insides in her eyes.

"Mom, I do not want to kill myself."

And when I say it, I know that I do not. I want that peace and power that Grace had, though. She was sure. She did not question. She knew herself and did not change for anyone, even though she was the butt of jokes. I just want to have her strength.

I have been reading about the Annunciation. I am trying to understand what Mary was like before she became the mother of Jesus. No one ever talks about what she did, or what her relationship with Joseph was like before she was pregnant with the son of God. Did she go to school? Did they make out? All that. Also, was she Jewish? I am learning from scratch. I am trying to find texts outside of the Bible that tell me more. These are the questions I have for Mrs. Adams, but she knows less than I thought. She has the scriptures down and all, but really, I am more interested in the people. No one seems to know how old she was exactly, but she was definitely a teenager, maybe even fourteen or fifteen. Now on Fridays, I go read in Grace's bed while the cake is baking, and I often fall asleep. The first time I got in Grace's bed in the afternoon, I was testing to see if Mrs. Adams would object. I smelled the cakes baking while I read the New Testament. Soon I was asleep, and I did not wake until it was dark. They left me alone. I was terribly embarrassed when I entered the kitchen and Mrs. Adams and Patrick were eating leftover lasagna at the old oak table.

"Oh, you're up! I didn't want to wake you, you looked so comfortable. Was it a good nap?"

"I am so embarrassed. I had no idea I would fall asleep for so long."

"You must need it."

"I slept so soundly. I can't believe it's dark."

"Don't worry. I called your mother."

"Oh thanks."

Patrick raised his head and looked at me as if for the first time ever.

"Hi, Patrick," I mumbled.

"Hey Eve."

It was awkward. Patrick was the most popular high school junior. He used to have girlfriends and athletic practices every day, and games. Now, I had heard he was not dating anyone, hadn't since the accident, and refused to do much other than workout in the gym and play soccer. His mother was worried that he talked so little, and brought no one home anymore, even though she was not fond of his girlfriends. Unlike Grace, he has never been so devout. He was a good Christian for his parents, but once he left fifth grade and found his own group, he kidded Grace about her devotion. He was nice enough to her, but he was clearly bothered by her weirdness too. She embarrassed him. He told her she needed to lighten up. She was fond of rolling her eyes at Patrick. Once I asked her if she liked having such a popular brother. She said she figured people were nicer to her than they otherwise would be. "Even though they call me a Jesus freak, they don't beat me up. It's probably because of Patrick."

There were pictures of them all over the halls from when they were little. One picture stands out. It was probably taken when they were about one and two. They are asleep. Their heads are touching, and Grace's tousled waves are curled around Patrick's head so that you cannot tell whose hair is whose. Their eyes are closed, and they both have the same rosy mouth. They are angels. Sleeping angels. It is the kind of picture you would see on a card and not believe it was real, real children that is. I wish I had a copy to look at. It makes me feel good. It makes me wonder if Grace's fate was planned from before her birth, that she was already an angel, and now she has returned to her real purpose.

"You look different," Patrick said.

"I do?"

"Yeah."

"She's so thin," said Mrs. Adams.

"I've been running more," I shrugged.

"Yeah, maybe that's it. Your face looks different."

"She's so pretty," smiled Mrs. Adams.

"Oh no . . . you don't have to say that. I'm half asleep. I guess I better get home," I said, flushed with embarrassment.

"Don't forget your cake."

"Oh thanks. Bye."

"Eve?"

Mrs. Adams stood up and followed me outside the kitchen door.

"Honey, you can sleep in Gracie's bed anytime. You just come on over."

"Thanks, Mrs. Adams. I was so tired."

"I know. So am I. We both need to get some sleep."

I walked home, my heart thumping. Did she know? Was she telling me that she knew that I was in Grace's room all along? Was she giving me permission to come in the middle of the night? Even if she didn't, and it was a coincidence, she had said 'you can sleep in Gracie's bed anytime.' She had invited me. Now I only had to worry about my parents. I started leaving a note on my bed in case they came in in the middle of the night, so they would not panic right away. But I dreaded the day they found out. They would put an end to it, and I would never sleep again or dream.

I dreamed in huge, epic stories. They were like feature-length movies. I dreamed that I was kidnapped and living in a Tuscan farmhouse that was surrounded by sunflowers. When I tried to escape, I could not find my way out of the sunflowers. It was so beautiful that I didn't care if I got out, and I laid down and fell asleep in the flowers, but then the flowers became poppies like in the *Wizard of Oz*, and I was wearing that blue checked dress. I dreamed that Grace was living in a palace that had a tower like Rapunzel. She would lean over, and her hair would touch the ground. But I could not get in, and she would not let me climb her sacred hair. I dreamed that I was running across the country, and I never needed to stop. I could just go through each state one by one at a steady pace and get water along the way when people handed it to me in cups like in that movie with Tom Hanks. Once I dreamed I had straight hair. Once I dreamed I had black hair. Once I dreamed that I could fly and see into people's houses and down below the ocean. I saw whales and sharks, and then I saw the river, and at the bottom, the blue Dodge Durango. I saw the bubbles and the closed window, and I saw a hand that was white and pressed to the glass.

I sat upright. This time I was in my bed. The clock read 12:47 only. My heart pounded. I got up and went down the hall and out the door. I ran. I needed to run until I could stop seeing it. Was she waving to me? Was she trying to tell me something? I ran for 25 minutes and then I walked. I wasn't afraid of my neighborhood, even though I was in the dark alone. I passed the houses, all quiet. I ran on the sidewalks over past the school and then back. Then I walked until my heartbeat was slow and steady. Then I walked across the grass at 124 Tuttle Lane, and I opened the gate to the back yard and I turned the corner and stood at her window. I lifted the window and climbed in. Then I lowered it and I stood and listened for any sound at all. When there was nothing, I got in her bed, and I closed my eyes and I breathed in and out until I was fast asleep. This time I dreamed of white sheets hanging in the sun next to a blue ocean. I could hear the waves. I don't think a fire in that bed could have woken me up. But then I opened my eyes right at 4:54, right on time. I went back to my own bed. My mom came in to make sure I was awake at 7:00.

"Sleep well?"

If she only knew I had been running and breaking and entering since she tucked me in last night. If she only knew what I dreamed. When I was in class after lunch, I often fought to stay awake. Everything seemed boring to me now that all I wanted to do was read the Bible and other books about it. I found a book called *Mary and the Annunciation*, that was only about that. Who was her family? What did she really look like? Was she anything like me? I was fifteen and my full height, yet I felt like I was shrinking, losing weight, and sinking into the background of life. I no longer raised my hand in class. The teachers notified my parents and we had a session with Dr. Phillips, a family session.

"I've been running more," I said about the weight loss.

"True," said my mother.

"Do you eat lunch at school?"

"Yeah."

"What do you eat?"

"Bananas, sandwiches, KIND bars, salad sometimes. I don't know."

"Do you eat in the cafeteria?"

"No."

"Why not?"

"It smells, and I don't like it."

"Where do you eat?"

"Outside under a tree. Or the library."

"With anyone?"

"Sometimes."

"Eve, do you think you are avoiding people?"

"No, I just like to be outside, and I like to read and eat my banana under a tree. I'm around people every minute of the school day. And I prefer the sofas in the library. A lot of people eat there."

"OK. Why are you running so much?"

I rolled my eyes. "I have been running since before the accident. I just find it easy now."

"Do you want to be thinner?"

"I'd rather be thin than fat."

"But do you think about being thinner?"

"I don't have an eating disorder. I eat when I am hungry, and I eat what I want."

"Eve, it would be understandable if you wanted to . . .

disappear, sometimes."

"Understandable, maybe, but not true," I said. "This is a waste of time."

"Your parents have the time. I have the time. So, you mean it is a waste of your time?"

"All of our time."

"What would you rather be doing?'

"Homework, cello practice, running, reading, eating, sleeping . . . see I am very well rounded."

She smiled and my mother wrinkled her brow. My father sighed. "I'm really okay," I said.

CHAPTER 4

Gaby

There was a new girl in orchestra. Her family was transferred to Bend Hill from Brazil. Her name was Gaby Drake. She played the viola and the cello, and she was better than me. I got to know her because we were paired up to do a duet for a state competition. I had a feeling there were adults behind this match, as she was forced to take the violin part, which would have been Grace's. I felt sorry for her because she was being used for my benefit. She had been told of the violist who had died tragically in a car accident. She didn't know that Grace was my one and only friend. I refused to give details other than that she drowned in the river, and she had been my partner last year in the competition.

"God, that's the most horrible thing I've ever heard," she said.

"Yeah. Do you speak other languages?" I asked, changing the subject.

"French and Spanish, some Portuguese."

"God," I said. "What don't you do?"

"We have lived all over, and my parents don't allow us to

watch TV," Gaby shrugged. "I had a lot of time on my hands when I was younger. I spoke Spanish first, then English in preschool. Then we lived in France for two years and I learned French. None of it was even taught to me. When we were homeschooled in South America, we all took a lot of music. So . . . that's it."

"You were homeschooled?"

"Yeah, it was safer. We had a tutor and a music teacher. We cooked a lot."

"You cooked for school?"

"No, we just cooked to eat. We did the lessons in about four hours and then there was the rest of the day . . . and no homework. Also, there was a big meal at midday every day. It was pretty nice, actually."

"Sounds like paradise. Brazil, no school. Do you hate this place?'

"Not yet. I like seeing the people and the way they dress. We were always alone, just my sister and brother and me. We went to town with our parents, but we were not really social with the kids, because there was a lot of danger."

"Was there a beach?"

"Oh yeah, we had a house overlooking the water. That was paradise. But we couldn't go down to swim alone. We had a guard with a rifle."

"Crazy . . . how'd you get here?"

"They were tired of the danger. And my dad finally got a transfer. We won't be here long. He builds computer stations, in rural areas usually."

"Couldn't you be homeschooled here?"

"Of course, but I wanted to go to school."

"I can't imagine. I want to stay home and read. I could learn everything by reading."

"What are you reading?"

"*Ordinary People.* I'm almost done. Sometimes I read the Bible."

"Are you in an organized religion?"

"No. I am sort of Jewish and nothing, actually. You know, my dad is Jewish, my mother isn't religious."

"Do they want you to read the Bible?"

"No. They think it's weird."

"I read it when I was in Brazil. We went to services in the Catholic church. I got into it when I had nothing else to do. See, being here there are so many distractions. I don't know how anyone reads anything."

"Which part did you read?"

"Oh, I just followed the service. I jumped all around." Gaby got off the bed and picked up her socks and pajamas from the floor. She threw them in the closet and shut the door before her mother came to the door and wrinkled her brow.

"Gaby, have you offered Eve a drink?"

"Not yet. We'll come out in a second."

"We have lemonade. And Gaby, that desk! You can't learn anything in that mess."

Gaby rolled her eyes when her mom walked down the hall. But she started throwing away the trash on her desk.

"My mom hates messes."

"Are you Catholic?" I asked.

"My mother is. So, I guess so, but we are not much of anything either. I don't buy into a lot of it. I think there is God, whatever you want that to be, and that's about it. I'm not really Christian."

"What about Jesus?"

"Well, he may have walked the earth and all, but I think he was just a man. I'm not very good at accepting things that are not logical at all. Even though I can accept God, I don't think it's a he who gave us his son and all that. Definitely not an old man. And of course, I believe in evolution. I think there is a good reason for faith, but really, I believe God is based in science, like the atmosphere, kind of, but with wonder and awe. I think the community and the music part of religion is good though. And it serves as a nice worldly glue," Gaby said. She talked like no teenager I had ever met.

"I want to believe it," I said. "If this is all there is, I don't know what I will do."

Gaby looked at me hard.

"This is high school in a small town. This is not all there is. Trust me, it's a great world out there."

"I need to get out more," I groaned.

And so, we practiced our duet, me knowing that Gaby could do a much better job on the cello. But we got it down, and won Superiors, and were chosen to go to music camp in North Carolina for several days. My parents were torn between concern as to whether I was ready to go away and being giddy with the prospect of me frolicking with other teenagers. Dr. Phillips felt I should do it. I knew that the chaperones would be advised to check on me often. The thing was that I wanted to get out of town really badly. I wanted to pick Gaby's brain some more as she was a wealth of information and might even be a real friend, and I wanted to see the mountains in North Carolina. But I did not know if I could go for days without sleeping in Grace's bed. I was afraid I would not be able to sleep at all, or worse, that I would lose the connection to her and to whatever I had felt in her room. My dreams there were real, and they saved me. How could I leave that and risk that it might not be there when I returned? I was in a near panic when I had to commit. It was Gaby who told me I needed to go. I had no choice. I needed to expand to be able to know God. God was not in Bend Hill, alone, she said. She did not know that maybe He was in Grace's bedroom every night, and maybe that was the only place I would ever know Him.

"Think of the mountains. The waterfalls, the trees. If there is a God, he or she is in the mountains."

But I was afraid He might not know where I was.

I had not told Gaby of my dreams or my thoughts about Jesus and Mary. She knew I was trying to make something of God and religion and all. I told her I was not sure I even believed, but this is what I felt since I had lost Grace. She was versed in philosophy, as her parents held discussions with their children on everything, so she explained the basics to me. We were alike in that no one else at Bend Hill High would indulge me on religion, and Gaby could talk about anything. Gaby liked being the teacher, and I gladly took the role of her student. I could talk almost without editing. She did try to steer me toward Buddhist and Tao ideals, the Old Testament, and I kept going back to Mary and Jesus, but I listened to it all. My parents were so happy that I had a new friend. I kept up with my Friday afternoons at the Adamses', baking cakes and reading. Sometimes on my run, I stopped in and delivered herbs from my mother's garden to Mrs. Adams. This was my thanks for letting me break into their house regularly.

I had dinner with the Drakes one night and was startled by the intensity of the table talk. These were people who took their dinner conversation seriously. They had an agenda, and topics to cover. They wanted to know what I knew, and I felt like a moron. Gaby's older brother and sister were every bit as bright and accomplished as she was. They spoke in English for my sake.

Gaby told them of my interests in Christianity, and her mother chose a passage to speak about. Her father was a scientist and debated the matters. I had broken out in a light sweat by the time we finished the meal. Her brother played the piano and her dad showed me his powerful telescope. I felt like I had landed in a foreign country. I expected a chess match next, or poetry by the fire.

After that night, I made excuses about returning. I didn't

feel up to it, for now. I invited Gaby to my little dinner table where we usually threw a salad together and ate in a variety of shifts and ways. My parents were so thrilled that Gaby was joining us that my mom made a menu, and asked if there were things she didn't eat. We were all out of whack. I felt almost as foreign at my table as at hers. But my parents were kind and very curious about all Gaby had to say, and I was soon able to sit back and enjoy the new pasta dish and the fresh bread from the bakery. Gaby had them enthralled. We got onto the subject of the trip, and they all ganged up on me and convinced me to go. I wanted to see the mountains and perform the piece. I just kept thinking about the nights I would be away from Grace's bedroom. I didn't know what I would do at night, maybe climb the highest peak, and see Him there. I soothed myself with the idea that God was in the heavens and the heavens were closer to the mountains. I signed up, my parents beaming as they wrote the check.

CHAPTER 5

North Carolina

S ometimes in Grace's bed, I would hear a noise and my heart would race thinking Mr. or Mrs. Adams would find me. I would say to myself, 'no more, this is the last time.' But then I would hear nothing, maybe I had imagined it, and soon I was sleepy again, and I closed my eyes and dreamed of the water, the river, icy and clean. The moss was a bright glowing green in my dream, and I was swimming like a seal, romping in the water, happy and full of energy. Then my eyes settled on a gold glint. I saw it resting on the bottom, on a rock. I reached for it. Her cross. Her necklace. When I reached, it fell away. I had no hands. I was a seal and though I could see it, I could not get it. I could not have her necklace. I woke breathing hard, frustrated, and sweaty. I was not calm and relaxed like I was usually. I got up and left earlier than usual. I fell into my own bed and slept until my mother was bending over me. "Eve, you overslept. It's late, hon."

We were leaving for the trip immediately after school and I had my bags packed and placed by the door. My mother made a real breakfast of toast and a fried egg and sat down with me while I crammed it down. I was not a morning eater, but she was so eager to sit with me, I ate anyway. She told me to slow down, that I could be late for school.

"Do you have your toothbrush and conditioner?"

"Yeah," I said.

"Do you think you'll be able to run there?"

"I brought my shoes."

"Dad and I stayed in Asheville two years ago, remember I told you about the Biltmore?"

"Mmmmhmm. All the rooms."

"Are they taking you to see it?"

"I don't think we have enough time. Between practice and performance, and the outdoor activities . . . I think there is a field trip, though, so maybe."

"Are you and Gaby ready?"

"Oh yeah. As ready as I can be. I hope I don't choke."

"I'm sure you'll be great."

I hugged them and said I would call from the bus. They insisted I check in. I was actually feeling good about going away for three days. I felt the freedom seeping into my skin as my mother drove away from the school. I had a whole long bus trip to sleep and listen to music, or chat with Gaby about things. I hoped I could run among the green, tall trees and rest on a mossy stone. I had seen pictures. My family took trips to a lake in the Adirondacks every summer. We had visited the Grand Canyon, and Bryce Canyon and San Francisco and Chicago, and even Colorado where there were bigger mountains. My parents had nearly bought a house in Napa Valley, and then reconsidered. We went to Florida, and the Bahamas and Paris, but we had never gone to North Carolina. We had never been to the South, actually. I liked to read books by Southern authors: Faulkner, and Eudora Welty. We read these books in my Honors English class in ninth grade. It made me want to see Mississippi. For my birthday we had planned a trip to New Orleans, but there had been a flood and we didn't get to go. After that, Grace died, and we never talked about New Orleans again. I wanted to hear the drawls and eat beignets in the humid, salty air. I really liked hot weather as much as I liked the cold crisp falls in the East. I was easily adaptable, I guess. I could live anywhere. I would check North Carolina out for future reference.

Gaby and I sat together on the bus, and she broke out a Ziploc bag of her mother's brownies. It reminded me of cake day. I was missing Mrs. Adams already, and she would be baking without me. I nibbled the brownie and closed my eyes imagining the batter and the spatula. I was the stirrer. I could smell the kitchen. I pulled myself together and concentrated on each bite, the chocolate, the egg, the flour, the sugar.

"She uses sour cream, doesn't she?" I asked

"Yeah, secret ingredient. How did you know?"

"I can taste it."

"You must be super sensitive."

"I guess."

We arrived late at night. The bus climbed a windy road up the side of a mountain until it stopped at a grassy field that was black as velvet. We had been instructed to bring flashlights and we all used them to get out of the bus with our bags. There was a central hall where we all met, and names were called and attached to cabin colors. Gaby and I were Forest Green. So were twelve other girls. We headed over and claimed a bunk bed in the far corner of the room. There were seven lined up against the wall and an open space on the left of the long room. Each bunk had a trunk at the foot where we could store our things. There was a braided rug between each set of beds. Something about the space, the order, the clean wood smell, the whitewashed walls, and the white metal beds made me feel like we were sloppy, greasy puppies in from the mud, ruining everything as we spilled into it. It was like a chapel in the woods, white and woody and spare. I didn't want it ruined by my teenage peers. I cringed and carefully arranged my belongings in the trunk, keeping everything neat in our corner. Gaby followed my lead, though she was clearly planning to dump her bag on the floor like the rest. She took the top bunk, and I was thankful for the bottom in its cozy cocoon-like way. Even the underside had been kept free of graffiti and gum, and was a smooth plank with a tiny inscription that read, "We cherish our cradles. Please keep them clean, and you will have sweet dreams."

Then there was a poem about dreams. I was touched by the care and thought that went into a camp retreat for ungrateful teenagers. When the lights were out, and I could open my eyes and see only black, the same as if they were shut, I was happy.

I had been so worried that I would wake in the night and panic without a place to go, but I woke to the sound of girls stirring and a door slamming. I had slept through the night. I felt my heart quicken. Had I lost my connection to God already? I was groggy and sluggish getting ready. It was as if all that lost sleep had caught up with me on this day, and I could have gone back to bed and slept another day and a half. We ate in the dining hall and were given the schedule of the day which included a brisk hike on a trail behind our cabins right after breakfast. I drank coffee and perked up a bit.

Gaby and I were buddies, of course, and we walked side by side up the mulchy path until we entered a sweet, little, rusty iron gate where the path narrowed. We were clearly ascending quickly, and people were breathing harder. My constant running kept me in good stead. Gaby was not in great shape. She was from a family of intellectuals, and they placed far more emphasis on words and music than exercise. In fact, only her sister, Gemma, had ever done anything athletic; she was a tennis player. So, Gaby huffed and puffed pretty steadily and our conversation was limited. I took in the bright green ferns, the dark moss, and then the light, nearly chartreuse leaves on the tall, sky-reaching trees above. It smelled so fresh and clean. It really was spectacular. There was a rocky creek that ran beside us and grew narrower as we climbed. The kids were complaining and demanding a break until our leader stopped at a fork in the path and told us to take the left and sit down on the logs. The logs were arranged in a circle and were two deep; actually it was more of an octagon. They handed out water bottles and we drank and listened to a short history of the area while Eric, the leader, stood in the center, where a fire had obviously burned recently.

"We roast marshmallows here. And tell ghost stories."

"How do you get here in the dark? It must take forever!"

"We come up early with sleeping bags, and camp."

"This must be creepy at night."

"Aren't there bears?"

"We keep a fire going and get rid of all the food. That's the key."

"Where are we going?"

"It's about another quarter-mile is all. It's worth it."

So, we continued walking, and as we reached the top, the trees opened up and, as if we were entering a kingdom, there were gasps of awe. We seemed to be at the top of the world. There was nothing higher than us. Far below was an enormous lake. All 36 of us, and Eric, spilled like baby blocks across the grass. It was a *Sound of Music*, Maria on the hill, twirling and singing with arms outstretched moment. No one complained or even sat down. The whole group, even Gaby, was rejuvenated and leapt with joy. The two of us walked over to one side and I held my arms out and closed my eyes. God. God was in the mountains. I knew then why I had come to North Carolina to play my cello. For the first time in a long time, I felt happy.

The walk back was easier, or at least the group was in better spirits. It seemed to go fast. When we came to the fork again, I asked what was on the path to the right, as it seemed dark and narrow. "Oh, that's another good one," Eric winked. "We may tackle that one Sunday." The remainder of the day we did what we came to do. We met the other school kids in a barn-like building and were formed into an orchestra. We were given music and a hard-driving conductor who hammered the kinks out of the pieces in a few hours. These were no slouches. These kids were the cream of the crop, and we sounded pretty good by dinner. The late afternoon was for us to work on our duets and have a rest before the evening show. Gaby and I were as good as we were going to get, so after an hour of practice, I was itching to get out of the room and into the woods. I was dying to run. Gaby was drowsy and I suggested she take a nap while I took off.

"Are you allowed?"

"No one said I couldn't."

"Where are you gonna go?"

"I'll take the path we took this morning. It's perfectly marked. I can't get lost."

"Well, don't go anywhere else. You could get lost and there ARE bears. Make noise."

"I will. I won't be long."

"I'll send someone after you if you don't return by 5:00, all right?"

"I'll be back. Remember I came here to see the mountains?"

CHAPTER 6

The Waterfall

T he path began not fifty paces from our cabin's back door. I stretched for a few minutes and then started off. When I entered the little gate, I closed it behind me and then I started to run. It was not really running, as it was uphill on a narrow path, and I was kind of chugging along. As I went ahead, the ground became damp and the sound of water, louder. Then, mud caked my shoes and I had to pull myself up onto some rocks by grabbing branches to keep going. When I got scared, I looked up and there was light again, and those layered leaves reaching up, up and up. I took the path to the right that we had not attempted. It was narrower, but I kept on. Just when I struggled with a slippery rock and an uphill leap, that I had to use my hands to recover, I pulled myself up onto what looked like a rock table, and I gasped. On the far side, crashing in front of me, was a waterfall.

I looked around to see if anyone was with me. I couldn't imagine I was the only one here to witness this beauty. But it was me alone. Me and the waterfall, and a black perfectly round pond between us. I noticed that my legs were streaked with mud all the way to my thighs. I was also sweaty, and wet from the mist. I was hot and my heart beat fast. I took off my shoes and socks and placed my foot in the water up to my ankle. It felt so good and cold, I leaned over and splashed the water onto my calves. Then I did the other leg. It was not enough. I wanted to be in it. But I was afraid. I could not tell how deep the water was and it was black, black, black. If I had someone with me, I thought, it might not seem scary at all. So, I got up and crept around the rock until I was at the edge of the waterfall and I stuck in my hand. It was strong and foamy. I looked at the rocks beneath it and saw that I could get under it without being in the black hole that gave me chills. I looked around before I removed my t-shirt and shorts and left them on the rocks, then I slowly moved onto the shelf below the pounding water. I splashed and pulled the water toward me until I was soaked and shivering.

Then I wanted more. I didn't care who saw me in my underwear. I didn't care how deep the pond was. I stretched forward and got my head in the falls. I dangled my legs up to my thighs. I closed my eyes and felt the thunder surround me. I felt nothing, no fear or shame. I couldn't see. I was immersed in power. And then I saw His face, in front of me, but surrounding me too. It was the same face I had seen in my dreams in Grace's bed. It was the golden-brown eyes of the picture of the Jesus I knew, the delicate forehead, but with the long, black hair of Grace. Only it was a man's face, and I was in it, breathing it. It could only be Jesus here in the waterfall, where He had called me to find Him. I came to the mountains and here He was!

I do not know how long I was with Him there. I returned to myself when my body hit the water as I fell into the pond. My feet did not feel the bottom, and I swam up fast, and pulled myself out as there was a flash of movement near the path. Was it an animal? Had someone seen me? "Hello?" I called. I pulled myself out of the water onto the ledge and rinsed my hair again in the falls. I hurried to put on my clothes. Then I took my time with my shoes as I took in the beauty of the natural chapel I had found, the miracle I had experienced. I didn't want to leave, but I had no idea how long I had been gone. I would not tell anyone about this. It was all mine. No one would believe me anyway. When I came to the gate, Gaby was there waiting and drumming her fingers.

"I was giving you three more minutes. What took you so long? I was really worried."

"I'm sorry, Gaby. I didn't have a watch, and it was so beautiful. I found a pond and I rinsed off. Anyway, I was fine. It's not that far. It was just uphill, you know, and I got hot."

"Well, we have to set up and then go to dinner. Everyone's in the barn. You better change quick."

"Gaby, remember you said God is in the mountains."

"Yeah."

"I know. I know what you mean."

"Aren't you glad you came?"

"Oh my God. You can't imagine."

After the show that night, we had a campfire and roasted marshmallows, the usual campy stuff. I was far away, thinking only of the waterfall and my pond Jesus. One of the counselors was the designated storyteller, and he told a sort of historical ghost story about the area. I was able to drift off and imagine the round blackness of the pond and the water crashing onto my head and washing me with God. I wanted to tell everyone, yet I wanted to keep it all to myself. In the past I had always been at a distance from His face, and I could barely make out His features, beyond Grace's magnificent hair, and the fact that He was a man. But this time, He was before me, and if I had turned around, He would have been behind me too. He was all around me and He felt familiar. I knew Him like I knew my own face. All the features were ones I recognized: the eyes, the forehead, the nose, the lips. I was all confused about why He looked so much like Grace, but not. Had Grace died so that I would know God? Was God Grace? Was her whole purpose in life to show me? Maybe our friendship, our sisterhood that I did not think I could exist without, maybe it was all to bring me here to meet God because of her, and to believe. I had come to the water like Grace had, and while she got death, I got this gift.

I felt tears fill my eyes and I quickly wiped them with my sleeve in the dark. The fire was getting lower, and the marshmallows were gone. I picked the hard brown-black edges off mine and then stuck my finger in the pure white goo beneath it. I sucked it off until my finger was clean and tossed the rest in the pit. It occurred to me that roasted marshmallows really didn't taste good. It was the experience of being in the dark and the licking flames, and the idea of cooking your own dessert in that flame on a stick, that was delicious.

Gaby wanted to chat. She had listened to the story and found the facts about the area interesting. I let her talk as I had not heard most of the story. She noticed I was quiet.

"Are you okay?"

"Yeah, I'm just so sleepy. That run wore me out."

"You said you saw a pond. Do you think it was the Black Pearl, the one he was talking about?"

"Huh?"

"The deep one?"

"I . . . I don't know. It was just a dark pond."

"He said it's bottomless. And it is a perfect circle. And people have seen spirits." I raised my head.

"I was falling asleep out there. What spirits?"

"He said it was Cherokee sacred ground. There was no explanation for the extreme depth, and that people had witnessed spirits. They prayed there. I want to find it. He didn't want to say where it was."

I was so torn between telling Gaby everything and taking her there, and not letting her in on my secret. I wanted to keep it mine. I didn't tell her. I slept hard again that night. I dreamed that I was swimming again. That black water was back and this time it frightened me. I could not see ahead. It was clean and soothing right where I was, but I could not see in front of me, and I felt panicked. Every now and then I saw a glint, a flash, and then I woke up. It was early in the morning, and everyone was sound asleep. I felt myself wanting to be at the waterfall. I was scared to go in the dark. But I wanted to be there. After laying there a while I got out my flashlight, and I got up. As I was closing the door, I heard a voice.

"Wait, I need to go too."

And one of the girls, Jill Benjamin, joined me. We walked to the bathrooms, and I abandoned my journey, and climbed back in my bunk. I lay there for a while. I imagined the climb through the wet branches, the black night making it impossible to see, and the rocks and debris making it hard to hang on to a flashlight. I thought of animal sounds and bears and ghosts and still, I wanted to go. I had to go. Today was the day we performed our duets, so there would be a block of time where we were free, and the others were playing. I would slip out without telling Gaby. I would leave a note. Now I wasn't afraid of the dark water at all. I had been there in my dreams. I drifted back to sleep trying to bring back His face. The mouth was so familiar. Who was this man? Was I in love with God, Jesus, a dream, a ghost, Grace? Was I crazy? So what if I was.

At breakfast, they gave us the itinerary for the day. We were to do some group games after breakfast, get some exercise and then hike to a lake where we would have a picnic lunch. After that, we had an hour to rest, and then the duets were scheduled every fifteen minutes. At four o'clock, we would board a bus and go to the Biltmore before dinner, and then back for the last campfire. It was a packed day. I was worried. The hour of rest was right before the duet. I would be pressed for time. Could I run up and maybe find a watch? Or could I request the first duet time? I decided to let the day unfold and do what I had to do. The games were silly and irritating for pretty much everyone. They were too forced, and we were all glad to move on to the lake hike. It was very different from the woods. It was through a wide meadow and then a patch of fern-covered forest and out onto a large dark blue lake with a sandy edge and a pier with cranberry-colored canoes tied to it. There were picnic tables under the trees. Pretty, but not spectacular like the first day. After we ate turkey sandwiches and fruit and cookies, we were allowed to get in the canoes, two at a time. We had to take turns. I was getting itchy, feeling the time slip away. But I paddled out and breathed in.

"You're so quiet," Gaby said.

"I'm just taking all this beauty in. I just don't want to forget this."

"I like it here too. I could live in North Carolina. It's so . . . green and gentle."

"Compared to what?"

"Harsh New England weather, Colorado mountains, the desert."

"Yeah, gentle. I like gentle," I said. But I wasn't feeling gentle, I was feeling wild.

Our duet was to be right in the middle of the allotted time. If

I left during the rest hour, I had almost two hours to be back, but Gaby would freak. If I waited until after, I would have no time. When we were in the bunks and Gaby pulled out her book, I pulled out my shoes.

"I need to move. I'm going for a walk."

"No way. You don't have time."

"I have almost two hours."

"Eve, we have to get our stuff together. You have a little over an hour and yesterday you were late."

"I'll take your watch."

"I'll go with you."

"I want to run. I'll be back in plenty of time and then I'll be relaxed. Gaby, you're acting like my mother."

"Well, you're not supposed to be alone, and this is about me, too. It's the duet."

"I promise I'll be back." She threw her watch at me.

I slipped through the gate and ran. I looked back a lot, but my heart was pumping, and I was quickly up the incline and into the thick steep part of the path. I had to hurry. I grabbed at the trees and pulled myself up and over the rocks. I kicked rocks out of my way. I finally got to the last part, and I climbed the awkward steps until my head was at the top of the ledge, and there I saw the thundering waterfall and below it a head. A person was there alone. It was a dark head. Looked like a boy, and he was treading water in the black hole, dipping his head into the falls. I watched. I was devastated. I thought it was mine. I thought it was scary and holy, yet here was a boy playing. I stayed as still as I could, only my eyes peeked above the ledge. I couldn't leave and I couldn't go further. I was a voyeur. Then, after a long while, as my calf began to cramp, he swam through the falls, and I saw that he was going to climb out onto the ledge that I had perched under. I ducked below and slipped down the path making as little noise as I could, tackling the brush. I had the adrenaline of a racehorse, and I was back at the gate in no time. I walked the perimeter of the campsite until my heart slowed. When I entered the cabin, Gaby was polishing her viola. "See, no problem," I said, and tossed her the watch. She raised her eyebrows.

"You've got mud all over you."

"Yeah, I didn't take the time to rinse. I'm going to run to the shower."

While I stood under the hot drippy water, I cried. I watched the mud and tears and water swirl around the drain. I was going to get back to my haven in the North Carolina woods one more time. I was not leaving in the morning without sitting under the falls again. I put my obsession aside for the duet. I curled myself around my cello and played as if it was my one true love. The piece was simple but powerful, and we received a Superior rating. It was over. Gaby hugged me; she was so happy. We boarded the bus for the tour of the house with the 250-something rooms. There was the typical chatter about our performances.

"I choked. I blew it," one said to another.

"No, you did not."

"Yes, I did. I got stage fright."

"You were fine."

"It was the best I've ever played, but my piece was so easy."

"My piece was way too difficult. We should have picked something easier. I screwed up a couple of times."

"It's just one stupid duet. It's not on your record or anything."

"I wanted a Superior."

Blah blah blah. They chattered on and on even though it was behind them, and no one really cared anymore. We tromped through the Biltmore and I was struck by the gardens, and the trees, more than the rooms. It was just wonderful, all that land. I was just in love with North Carolina. I felt there was something vibrating in me. I decided I must have lived there in a former life. After we ate at a pizza restaurant and then gathered around the fire for our wrap-up and instructions, we headed back to the cabins. I divided my dirty clothes into darks and lights as I always had, separated the few clean things, and placed them all in my duffle. My cello was already in the barn waiting to be packed in the bus. I put my clothes out and had my running shoes under the bed. I was sleeping in a t-shirt and shorts. Everyone seemed tired and cranky, and no one was for staying up all night. I read a bit and then the counselor came by and called lights out. It was eleven o'clock and everyone was ready. Everyone but me. I had my flashlight under my bed. We were to get up at seven. No one ever got up early. I so wanted to be there when the sun came up. If I could get Gaby's watch, I could time it and be back for the wake-up bell. Yet I was so anxious, I thought I might have to go right then when I was sure everyone was asleep. I pictured His face, my own personal Jesus, and it calmed me down.

While I was lying there, I saw what I needed. Across the room, on the trunk at the foot of Jill's bed—her watch, I guessed. I got up and crossed the room on tiptoe and scooped it up. I crawled back into my bunk and held it to my beating heart. I closed my eyes and willed myself to sleep and then to wake up on time. It was a fitful night. I did not dream. I kept waking up and straining to see the watch. Twice I turned the flashlight on under the bed. Finally, it was 4:30 and I made myself lay there until 5:00. Then I got up and got the flashlight and my shoes and I crept out the door where I was smacked by the damp air and the overwhelming blackness. I tiptoed down the steps and put my shoes on by feeling around. I really couldn't see a thing. I slipped behind the gate and up the trail in a flash with that flashlight pointing straight down just in front of my shoes. I made it into the woods and then was alone with the trees and the night noise.

In my haste, I hadn't been afraid, and now I was away from the camp, alone in a forest where I couldn't see my hand in front of my face and the feathery leaves brushed my cheek and thighs. I swatted at imaginary bats and heard things that could be boys or bobcats or ghosts for all I knew. I was scared. I stood still and shined the flashlight around me until

I pulled myself together. I looked at the watch and told myself I had plenty of time. I would take my time and get there and relax, then the sun would rise and save me. I had come to know the trail in the daytime, but at night it was like doing it blind, and it was a different game. I only had a narrow beam from my flashlight, and I used it to place my feet. All the brush in front of my head was fresh and creepy as it swatted me and grazed me. Nevertheless, I kept on and the owl that cooed in my ear was my mascot. The sound of the falls was getting louder and louder, pulling me to it. Finally, I reached the ledge and I put the flashlight in my teeth as I used both arms to pull myself up. When I was safely perched and the thunder of the water drowned out any other sound, but terrified me in that blackness, as if it was devouring me, I took the light and shined it around. I was alone here at last.

Once I asked Grace why Jesus was such a big deal. I understood the God thing, but Jesus was just a man. What did it matter if God had a son and if He was a selfless, pearl of a soul? So what? So was Mother Teresa. Why was Jesus the key to the Christian religion? Wasn't God enough? She was patient with me. She resisted the urge to roll her eyes. She sighed a little and took my hands and looked me in the eyes. She leaned in until she was two inches from my face. Very slowly she said,

"He SUFFERED and DIED for our sins, mine, and yours. He died so that we could live eternally. Imagine that sacrifice. God created us in his image. Jesus died for us and gave us eternal life. He is the reason for Heaven, so we have NOTHING to fear, not even death."

"Oh," I said. I still didn't understand what made her believe that, but I did not ask for more.

"You have sins?" I asked. I found that ridiculous. Grace was pure as the day she was born.

"We all have sins, Eve. We are born in sin."

"How is that?"

"Adam and Eve were not satisfied with God. They broke the simple rules, and all of their children forevermore are born to sin because of them. That's why we get baptized, to relieve us of original sin."

"Okay, that is just weird," I said.

"Maybe. But it is true."

I thought about my biggest sin. I wasn't saved. I let her go to the play without me. That day she had gotten on my nerves. I told her my mother wouldn't let me go. But I lied. I really just didn't want to go.

I looked at Jill's watch and it was 5:41. It was light enough to see my surroundings. I removed the watch and my clothes and folded them up and placed them behind a rock where they wouldn't be splashed. I just wanted ten minutes in that downpour. I put my feet in and splashed water on my legs and shoulders. I shook with cold, but I spread my arms until I grasped the ledge firmly and could arch my back and head forward. The water hit my forehead and I gasped from the shocking cold. I nearly let go. Then it was spilling down me and I pushed forward until it was hitting me full on. I felt pressure on my shoulders, and then I saw. In my eyes that were closed, His hair was tangled. It was my hair too. All that hair was so wild in front of His face that I could not see Him. Yet He was so close. I chewed with my mouth, thrust my tongue, hoping to break through. I kicked. I panicked and finally, I reached with my hand to pull the hair free, and I lost my grip. I plunged down under the falls still grabbing at that long hair. I fought. Then I felt strong arms around me lifting me, warming me. The hair was free, and His eyes held mine. His lips touched mine. We were under the black water, but I could feel every part of Him, and I could breathe. He breathed for me. We were there, underneath, unseen, undressed. I had found Him. He saved my life.

CHAPTER 7

Naked Mountain Girl

W hen they found me, I was in the dirt behind the ledge. I was unconscious and blue-lipped in my underwear. The counselor carried a blanket and he covered me, until they came with a stretcher and took me out of the woods. I was in the Asheville hospital for two days, where they stitched my cut, treated me for hypothermia, and gave me a complete psychological evaluation. Of course, my parents had come. The orchestra had gone back to Bend Hill on the bus. But I got to stay in North Carolina. I felt fine—wonderful, in fact. I was in love.

I told them I had found the pond on a run and had been there twice. I knew the trail, and that night I couldn't sleep, so I decided to go to watch the sunrise there before wake-up. I must have fallen against the rocks. I couldn't remember anything else. But that was all. I just wanted to see the waterfall for the last time. They tried to pry it out of me. How did I find it? Had I heard the stories about the Black Pearl? They asked me if I heard voices, stuff like that. I know they grilled Gaby. My parents wanted to blame the chaperones, but it was hard when I had left the cabin in the middle of the night. They kept suggesting that my judgment must be critically impaired, as it was an extremely dangerous thing to do, especially in the dark. "I didn't know. I thought it would get light any minute. I just couldn't sleep. I had a flashlight. I'm sorry."

My parents took me home on a plane and I sat, bandaged on the head, and stared at the clouds. I had let them down. My first time away, and I had failed them. The look on my mother's face told me she wanted to believe I was healthy and strong. My adventure had been one of a curious insomniac, and that is all. But there was that question lingering, maybe I was impaired—my judgment was, surely—and maybe worse, maybe I was crazy. When I got home, I just wanted to sleep. If I couldn't go back to the Black Pearl, I wanted to find Him in my dreams.

I had been unconscious when Eric, the counselor, found me in the dirt, so I had not been embarrassed. When my parents arrived, I was a patient, not a half-naked girl. So, when I had to enter the halls of Bend Hill Senior High School, I experienced the first arrows of unwanted attention. I walked looking down and hugging the walls. All eyes were on me, that girl who was found in the dirt, naked, on the school trip . . . that crazy girl who took her clothes off in the mountains. God knows what stories were going around. When the few friends I had asked me directly, I said that I just fell into a pond and hit my head when I was on a run. It was no big deal. Then they asked why I was naked, of course, and I rolled my eyes as if that was so juvenile, and told them that I was in my underwear, and I was rinsing the mud off in a waterfall when it happened, and I lost my footing. My clothes were right beside me. I'm sure most fifteen-year-old girls could not imagine taking their clothes off beside a waterfall in nature, no matter how hot or muddy they were.

Anyway, the stories circulated, and I became a bit of a celebrity in the way that you least desire. Guys, stoners, and football players alike were intrigued, and the ones who were brave enough came up and whispered things as they passed me. "I like the mountains, too," "Skinny dipping is my best sport," "Come swim with me anytime." They passed me notes. They felt they had the right to touch my hair, my shoulder, and look me in the eye. My life as a nobody was over. I acted superior. I waved them away and went on with my day. When Taylor Watts leaned up against my locker as I was pulling my math textbook out and asked if I would go to a movie with him, I could not conceal my shock. I just looked at him, speechless. He was a popular jock, but one of the decent ones. He was a friend of Patrick Adams. He had blond wavy hair and blue eyes and long lashes. Even though we had taken swim lessons together as preschoolers, he did not know I existed until now.

"No, I doubt it," I stammered, clutching the book.

"Why not?" he persisted.

"I'm late for math," I said, slamming my locker shut, and I took off.

He caught up with me at lunch, where Gaby and I were eating at a table in the back of the cafeteria. He asked if he could talk to me alone for a minute. I huffed and said, "Okay," and I looked at Gaby, who stopped chewing her tuna sandwich and tilted her head up at Taylor. I very slowly put my fork down and pushed back my chair. I followed him to a corner of a hallway outside the cafeteria, where Gaby was still in the corner of my eye. My heart was thumping as I glanced around to see if Taylor's friends were watching. There was no one looking our way that I could see, aside from Gaby.

"Why won't you give me a chance?" he asked me.

I wrinkled my eyebrows. "How do you even know me?"

"I've noticed you around. You're Patrick's sister's friend."

"Patrick's sister is dead."

"I'm sorry. I just know you because of her, that's all."

"I don't know you," I said.

"You could try to."

I shrugged. "I'll think about it. My parents barely let me out of the house anymore," I lied. This would thrill them to no end.

"Well, parents like me," he said.

"I need to finish my lunch," I said.

"Ok. I'll call you then."

"Sure."

And I went back to Gaby, who looked at me as if for the first time.

"Taylor Watts. He . . . you know . . . I'm the naked mountain girl now," I said.

"Is that what he said?"

"No. He wants me to see a movie with him."

"And?"

"I said I'd think about it, but unlikely."

"He's thinking about you naked," Gaby said.

"I know."

I did not know Gaby the way I had known Grace. I could not tell if she felt sorry for me or disappointed in me, or was just worried that our relationship was changing. Grace would have shown it on her face. Gaby collected her garbage and changed the subject.

But I rattled on. "I'm not going. You know, it would be way too weird. Why would a person you don't know ask you to go somewhere with them?"

"Eve, that's how you get to know a person."

"No one goes on dates anymore," I said. "Right?"

"Apparently he does," she said.

"Let's go," I said, and we picked up our stuff and threw it in the garbage can.

My parents actually took care of that. As I suspected, my mother was delighted I had been asked on a date, but she was not going to allow me in the car with a sixteen-year-old. I was not allowed to date in cars. So, she suggested I invite him over. Or she would take us to the movie or drop me off. I rolled my eyes.

"I didn't want to go anyway," I said.

"Evie, come on. You can meet up there. Or you can watch

a movie here. Dad and I will stay away."

"Mom, I was just keeping you up to date. I do not want to invite some boy over here that I do not know."

"Well, he sounds nice. I'm sure he would understand if I just dropped you off at the theater."

But I had a boyfriend in my head, or in North Carolina or in Heaven. When your boyfriend is Jesus, a high school boy just will not do. When I told Taylor that I was not allowed to go out, so he could go on with his life, he nodded.

"Can I call you?"

"Why?"

"To talk?"

"Look Taylor, I know why you want to get to know me. You're the only one brave enough to approach the naked mountain girl with the head injury. Listen, I don't regularly take my clothes off and swim in lakes around here. I had an accident while I was running in North Carolina. It's not going to happen again."

"Eve, I'm not like that."

"Yeah," I said.

"I'm going to call you," he said.

"Whatever."

And I was gone.

The funny thing was that the night I got back home from North Carolina, I slept until morning. I did not wake and go to Grace's bed. The night after that, I prepared myself to get up, and then I slept right through again. The thing was that I had dreams that fulfilled me in my own bed, and I did not need to go to Grace's room. It seemed that since I had been with Him in the pond, I didn't need to find Him at Grace's. He was with me all the time. I just wanted to sleep. I went to bed earlier and I slept later. I often took a nap instead of going running, and there were times I was barely able to keep my eyes open in class. I still ran in the evenings, but I seemed more sluggish. The adrenaline was not there. I used the time to daydream, but I ran out of steam, and my runs were shorter. I was going back to my old lazy style.

I still went over to see Mrs. Adams on Friday afternoons and baked. She was worried about my head. The word accident did not mean accident to her any longer. "Accident" meant dead. So, she reached out and touched my stitches, and pulled me to her. "You have to be more careful," she said. "I couldn't bear it if anything happened to you."

And that is when I knew that I was her last connection to Grace. She needed me more than her own family sometimes. Her husband's grief was inside. He turned to work. Patrick turned to lacrosse and the gym, and she was left standing in the kitchen with no one to even cook for. Other than her Bible classes, those Fridays were her salvation. So, we began to design Christmas cookies and we read the story of Mary and Joseph. Instead of candy canes and wreaths, we planned Wise Men and stars and barn animals. We were going to create a nativity and maybe shellac them for the tree if they turned out good enough. We were practicing. It was still October. But we had big plans. And Mrs. Adams had not gone through a Christmas without Grace. She had to keep busy. And I would help her.

When I envisioned Mary, I envied her simple life. No high school, homework or makeup, no loud popular boys in the halls. I imagined her stirring a pot or sewing her simple clothes by the fire. Then there was Joseph. Just what was their relationship before the angel came to her? Did they make out? Did they take walks together? Did their parents introduce them? Were they in love really, or did their closeness just speed up big time when the angel Gabriel came to Mary and said, 'and unto you a son is born . . . the son of God.' My God, what did she do first?

CHAPTER 8

Morning Sickness

T here had been nights where I slept through without dreaming, and nights where I had dreamed about being in the halls of high school with Gaby and Taylor Watts and math problems. I dreamed that I forgot about the science test and roamed the halls looking for the right door and all that. I had woken up and stumbled to the bathroom, too groggy to even imagine running or climbing into windows. But always I felt His presence there in the night. He was hovering. Sometimes I had real moments with Him, where he stroked my hair or covered me with His arms. It was never again like the morning at the waterfall, but He was clearly nearby. I was frustrated and soothed at the same time. I always woke up feeling blessed and tingly. But I was changing. Somehow, I felt my body had been taken over. All my wiry, jittery energy had left me. Instead, I was groggy and slow. I just felt different. My breasts were sore. My lips felt fuller. I wasn't hungry, but then I felt faint from not eating. My cello felt like it weighed more. Even Gaby noticed I was different.

"You seem so tired all the time."

"Yeah, I am. I feel so sleepy. I just want to sleep."

"Have you been to the doctor? You could have mono."

"Don't you have to kiss someone to get mono?"

"Nah," she shook her head.

When Taylor called, I talked to him. I thought about Joseph. He asked me questions about myself. I answered them. I yawned. He told me about his family and his friends. He and Patrick were on the lacrosse team together. He had been with Patrick right after the accident when he was trying to recover from the trauma.

"Patrick isn't the same anymore," Taylor said.

"Duh. He was the one who tried to save her . . . and couldn't," I said. "That would change anyone."

"He can't be still anymore. He keeps moving all the time. He has become our best player."

"I know how that feels, wanting to keep moving."

"You do too?"

"I did. I was running further and further and more often. Then I slowed down. Just recently. After I was in the hospital, I just calmed down. I can sleep now. In fact, all I want to do is sleep."

"Maybe you're getting over the grief. Maybe it's time."

I thought about it. If he only knew. If he only knew what I replaced it with, what I longed for, what I dreamed about. Not him and his long lashes. I wasn't like other girls. He was just a passing thought, a distraction in my, otherwise, loaded mind.

"What happened to Patrick's girlfriend?" I asked.

"Addie?"

"Yeah, I think so. She disappeared."

"She's still around. He refused to talk after Grace died. Even to her. She wanted to stand by him, but eventually, there was nothing to stand by. He removed himself from everyone."

"Even you?"

"Oh yeah, for a while. Now he talks to me some, but not about her. I think he is failing some classes, and his parents are freaking out. Once he told me he hated God, and he wants to shake his mother and tell her she should hate God. That's the most he ever said to me about it."

"Wow. She would be shocked. She would be devastated."

"That's why he hasn't done it . . . yet. He keeps a lot inside and I think it's really bad for him. He's really angry at her, though."

"He blames her?"

"Of course he does, even though it was just an accident, and he knows that. She made them go, and apparently, she had a migraine and still wouldn't let him drive. He needs to blame someone. But really, the problem is, I'm sure you know, he blames himself."

"Has he told you that?"

"In a way. It is all over him. He was the one who went after her and couldn't get her. He got his mother out first, so you know, he wishes he had gotten Grace. He was down there in the dark and he couldn't get to the car. Can you imagine what it was like?"

"Oh, believe me, I've dreamed it a million times."

"I think Patrick never sleeps. He might be taking something. If he doesn't sleep, he doesn't have to dream. He just keeps moving. I'm worried about him, and I don't think his parents get it. They think God will take care of him. Do you believe in God?" Taylor asked.

"Mmhmm. I do now. My parents have not really raised me to, but I do believe in something, and I believe Grace . . . " and then I stopped. I don't know why I was going on and on with this boy I hardly knew.

"Grace?"

I was silent.

"Grace is in Heaven?" he asked.

"I guess so. I have to believe she's somewhere good."

And then I changed the subject. Taylor Watts wasn't going to ruin my new love story with all his compassion.

Gaby and I started doing our homework together at my house after school. I think she liked being out of her very full house, and I felt better knowing that she didn't feel abandoned by me for the popular people. I felt like I was standing firm. I would not become one of them, just because they extended an invitation. I was better than them. Gaby and I—and somehow that included Grace—we were different, and we were going to stay that way. Also, Gaby was a great help when it came to my academic life. I would have taken a nap if she had not been there to prod me on the precalculus problems, and essay ideas on *The Canterbury Tales*. She knew she was taking the lead, and she liked it, and I was fine with it. Now I was not only sleepy, but nauseous a lot of the time. I wanted to live on toast with strawberry jam. My mother's frequent Thai dinners turned my stomach.

Dr. Phillips was interested. She scanned my face in that soft, eager way. She saw something but wanted me to be the one to reveal it. She had been seeing me twice a week since I had come home from North Carolina, but our relationship had shifted. I was not so secretive; I just tried to stay awake. So what if it slipped that I was way too interested in Jesus, and in Mary's love life. Big deal. What would she do? She realized I was far less edgy, and she got her foot in the door.

"Your mother says you were asked on a date."

"Yeah, she was over the moon. Then she wouldn't let me go. She wanted to have him over for tea and crumpets."

Dr. Phillips laughed. "I doubt that."

"It's true. Anyway, they were ecstatic. He's a popular boy, a jock."

"Well, well."

"You know why he asked me out."

"Because you're very attractive and cool, and sort of a jock too."

"Right."

"What do you mean, right? You're a beautiful girl, and a runner."

I rolled my eyes. "I am NOT beautiful, AND a runner and a jock are two VERY different things, and come on Dr. Phillips, you know the reason."

"You mean, why this is the first time someone has approached you?"

I wrinkled my brow and glared.

"You mean the incident on the trip made you . . . . stand out?"

"Yeah, specifically the naked part. I'm the famous skinny dipper. You'd be amazed at what that can do for your social life."

"Well, you are only fifteen, a sophomore. I think you would have been noticed eventually by the same crowd. The naked part just sped things up a bit," she said, smiling.

"I will never be one of them. I don't know what it was like when you were in high school, but there are very distinct groups. I am a cellist with messy hair and good grades in honors classes. And I don't worship boys in helmets. The naked thing has changed everything in my life."

"Is it a good change?"

"What do you think?"

"Well, you seem more relaxed, more happy even. I think it might be good, maybe just a little."

"They pass notes and whisper things to me in the halls. I just want to be left alone. It is not good."

"What about the guy who asked you out?"

"Well, he's nice enough. He's one of the better ones. He's popular enough to associate with me without risking his status."

"So, you talk to him?"

"Yeah, I have talked to him."

"Is that nice?"

"It's fine."

She looked at me without commenting.

"He's a friend of Patrick's. Grace's brother."

"Okay."

"So . . . he knows . . . some of it."

"So, you have someone to talk to about Grace."

"Well, a little."

She smiled.

"I think you're doing quite well."

"Yeah, so can I stop coming so often? This really cuts into my studying."

"I think so. We can cut back to once a week for now."

When I got up to go, I felt a wave come over me. I made it to the bathroom down the hall just in time to vomit in one great flood. I washed my face and saw that I was pale as milk. I looked different to myself, too. My mother was waiting downstairs. I wondered if I had a fever. The rest of the afternoon I took it easy. I didn't run. Gaby and I did math over the phone. But I felt okay, not really sick. I woke up, however, at dawn, and ran to the toilet again. Sitting on the edge of my bed, I touched my sore breasts. I had seen enough movies to know these signs. Could it be real? Was this part of the plan? Was I going to learn everything about Mary and Jesus by being Mary? Was I pregnant with the new Jesus? I shivered. I thought of Him wrapped around me in the black pond. I had not imagined it. I had not imagined Him. I was called to the waterfall in the middle of the night for a reason. Now what? If I thought being the naked girl was bad, how would they handle this?

It was only Wednesday, but I needed to see Mrs. Adams. I don't know what I was going to say to her. But I needed to see her to find out if she saw something different in me. I would try to run after school and stop by with basil and parsley. We still had pots of herbs growing under a lamp, even at this time of year. Maybe she could detect it. Maybe Mrs. Adams could spot a pregnant virgin right away and would know what to do. Maybe they discussed this sort of thing in Bible study classes. They might be looking for her and know just what to do when the next bride of God was near. When I approached the kitchen door of the Adams house (Grace and I had always used the back door, and I still did), I could see her in the window. She was preparing some kind of meat and watching the little TV. No one else was home. She was wearing her gray sweatpants that she did yoga in. I knocked quietly. She startled and then broke into a grin when she saw it was me.

"I brought some herbs," I chirped. "We're drowning in them."

"Evie, how nice of you! It's so nice to see your face in the middle of the week . . . and I can use those right about now. Ahh, they smell wonderful."

"What are you making?"

"Oh, some flank steak and mashed potatoes and salad. You want to stay for dinner?"

The thought of the hot food made my stomach lurch.

"I can't. My mom's got something cooking."

"How is she?"

"She's fine. Same old Mom."

"And Raine?"

"Good, I guess. I hardly ever talk to her."

"And what about you, Miss? Your cut is almost healed."

"Yeah, it was nothing, just a few stitches."

"Well, you are lucky you didn't have much worse. You were unconscious." She looked down. She was thinking of Grace. The idea of me near the dark water, unconscious, made her shiver.

"What should we attempt this Friday?" She looked back up and changed her face. I wanted to make her happy again. I wanted everything to be the way it was. How many cakes and cookies would it take to find Grace?

"Maybe something that will be ongoing," I said. "What about our nativity in a gingerbread house? The best one ever made. A big one. We can design it and bake a little each week."

"Oh, I don't know. I know you love the idea. I can bake, but I know nothing of designing and putting together a house."

"We can do it. I'll figure it out. We have lots of time. Not so much a house, but a shed, you know, a manger can't be too difficult."

"If you want. We can try. I wouldn't know where to begin."

"I'll find some books. I'll go online. We already figured out how to make donkeys."

She smiled. She would indulge me. She wasn't interested in the project, I could tell, but it would mean I would be around more. Just then Patrick burst through the door, sweating, even though it was probably fifty degrees outside. I blinked at the sight of him. We never looked each other in the eye because I was so shy around him, and I was just his baby sister's friend, of no interest. Now that she was gone, it was really awkward. We had only ever been in the same room because of Grace, and now she was missing. The elephant not in the room.

"Is it Friday?" he asked.

"Noooo . . . it's a mid-week treat." Mrs. Adams said. "Eve just brought me herbs from their garden."

"Well, it's not really a garden," I said.

Patrick was looking at me strangely, like he was trying to communicate something through his eyes. But he made me nervous, so I looked away.

"I heard you're talking to Taylor," Patrick said, opening the refrigerator.

"Um . . . well sort of. I've talked to him a couple of times."

"I think he likes you," he said. He wanted me to be nice to his friend. Mrs. Adams looked from one of us to the other, like a ping-pong game spectator. This was highly unusual, Patrick and I having a conversation.

"I don't think so," I said.

"Do I know Taylor?" Mrs. Adams interrupted.

"Taylor Watts, Mom!" Patrick groaned.

"Oh, the blond Watts boy. He's adorable. I remember him from Bible school."

"Mom, that was years ago. He's on the team with me."

"Oh, I know. I just think of him then, when he was so cute with those long eyelashes and curly hair."

Patrick rolled his eyes. I winced.

"Well, I gotta get home. It's getting dark."

"Thanks, Eve. You know I'm always happy to see you. Tell your mom thanks for the herbs."

"I will."

"Bye Eve," Patrick said, tilting his head as I closed the door.

I could tell they were talking about me as I left. When I passed the side of the house, I could hear their voices. Could they see something different about me? Mrs. Adams had looked different to me, actually. She was always the bright, adoring mother, the kind you see on TV unless, on the rare occasion, she showed her stern face. She was never moody or angry or disappointed, that I could tell. Her range of emotions was small compared to my mother's. She was almost creepy in that way. I always wondered if she had another side. Then after Grace died, she had a softer sadness about her. But she was still so kind, and even optimistic. Tonight, I had seen her look tired. Just like me. She seemed slower and worn around her eyes, defeated, like she wasn't sleeping. Wouldn't it be odd if now that I was sleeping in my own bed, she might be awake in hers? Or even wandering the halls or lying wide-eyed in Grace's bed? Maybe she knew I had been there all along, and now she missed me coming in the night. I could spin stories in my head all day. Who knew what Mrs. Adams thought? It had been seven months now, and her grief was just starting.

It had been nine weeks since my last period. This was not so unusual for me. I did not have periods like clockwork. I missed them occasionally, actually. But when I counted it up on the calendar after throwing up in the morning so bad I could not go to school, I knew I was going to have to buy a test and see. That part I could deal with. But then what? I had to make a plan. I needed to talk to someone, and Gaby was the only one. I was terrified to suggest to her that I was pregnant. She was a scientist at heart. And to her that would mean I had a life that I had kept secret from her. She would be hurt, or if I told her the truth, she would think I was crazy. Also, she would not seriously consider my Immaculate Conception. She was my only choice, though. I would certainly not tell my mother or Mrs. Adams yet. Or Taylor Watts. And my sister would laugh out loud. Maybe Gaby would do the research if I convinced her I was a virgin. There might be other ways to get pregnant. At least I was sure she wouldn't tell anyone.

CHAPTER 9

Parthenogenesis

I stood in the aisles of Walgreens, waiting for the people to clear. We always used Edward's Drugs for prescriptions and most everything else. It was much closer. But I ran the extra miles to get to the Walgreens in the next town over where I was not known. I grabbed the box with two tests and then covered it with an *InStyle* magazine and a Diet Coke and conditioner and Q-tips. The girl at the register didn't even look up when she scanned it. She just took my money and gave me change.

I couldn't really run home with the bag, so I walked and passed the park where I watched all the mothers and strollers and the toddlers in their fleece jackets and knit caps. I looked at the pregnant women. One looked regular, light on her feet—a woman who just happened to have a huge growth in front, like another head or something. The other looked heavy and lumbering, squishy all over, large. I wondered what type I would be. I was fifteen. I had the rest of the school year to deal with. What was I going to do? Maybe since I was so young, I would just be the small kind, not so noticeable under a big shirt. There was a girl in Raine's senior class in high school that was pregnant, and no one ever knew. She wore bigger clothes, and she didn't really show until the end. She had the baby at the end of winter, I think, and then she missed a few days of school, and she was back. It was really weird, I remember my sister saying. Apparently, few people knew, since she wasn't really the popular type. She just went to classes and then got out of there. And since she wasn't one of the "noticed" people, no one bothered to ask why her clothes had changed and she kept to herself. They were a Catholic family, and her mother raised the baby while she went to school. It was like it was the most normal thing in the world, like she had added an extra elective or another pizza topping. They said her boyfriend was not allowed to see her, but they snuck around at school, of course. And Raine said they were planning to get married after graduation. I don't know whatever happened. I wondered if Raine knew. Now I wanted to know.

But the truth was, she had been seventeen and almost done with high school, and I was only a sophomore. And, I had to remind myself, I was also a virgin. This was something that would not be kept quiet. When I eventually got to a doctor, surely, they would see that I was a virgin, and I was a freak of nature. Then I would have to deal with the interrogation and probing, I guess. They would send me away to await the birth and study me. And what if there were people wanting to get their hands on this new baby Jesus. Also, I don't think my mother is the type to take on a new baby now. Mrs. Adams might. She loves babies and she needs something to take up all her time.

"Gaby," I said the next afternoon while we did homework on my bed. "Something really strange is happening with me."

"What?" she asked.

"Well, I haven't had a period in a long time."

"Are you usually regular?"

"Pretty much, not totally, but it's been nine weeks."

"Well, are you worried?"

"Well . . . yeah."

"Oh?"

"Well, like I don't know what it could be. I feel tired all the time and my . . . boobs hurt. And . . . nausea."

"Jesus. Sounds like pregnant to me."

"But I can't be."

Gaby looked at me. She lifted her eyebrows.

"I haven't had sex."

"Well, then what are you worried about?"

"I have all those signs. I feel like I might be . . . isn't there some other way you can get pregnant?"

Gaby burst out laughing. "Didn't you ever get the talk, Eve? Didn't they go over this in fifth grade?"

"No, I mean like some weird hormonal fluke? Aren't there any cases of unexplained pregnancy?"

"Yes. The Virgin Mary," Gaby said, again with the eyebrows.

"Well, maybe it could happen again?"

She looked at me kindly, searching my face. Gaby bit her lip.

"I don't think so," she said.

"I know it sounds really weird, but I . . . things have been happening to me. I have these dreams that seem real, and I have these dreams about Jesus or God. I know, I know, it doesn't make sense, but in North Carolina, at the waterfall, I think something happened to me there. Gaby . . . you have to help me."

"Well, why don't you take the test first. You're probably not pregnant, and you're all worked up for nothing."

"And what if it's positive?"

"Then we'll go see a doctor."

"I'm afraid to take it."

"What's the worst thing that can happen?"

"That I'm fifteen and pregnant and no one believes me that I haven't had sex, and I'm carrying an alien that eats me alive from the inside . . . or some baby God."

"Okay, slow down. There is an answer. We just need to get to it. You're thinking you are like some modern-day Virgin Mary?"

"I don't know what I think."

"I think you are going to find out that you are not pregnant. Do you have a test?"

"It's in the bathroom."

"Go take it."

"I'm scared."

She grabbed my hand and pulled me off the bed. "Let's go." For Gaby, this was an adventure.

I took the first test. There was the faintest line. But Gaby said it probably didn't count. She kept the I told you so's to herself. I didn't feel any better. "Take the other one," she said, "then you'll be sure." When it was the same, I felt better, but that night in bed, I started to think. If this was a virgin birth, this would be no normal pregnancy, nor a normal baby. Science and at-home pregnancy tests were not going to solve anything. I was back to square one. I had forgotten to tell Gaby about the vomiting. Now that she knew my secret, I might as well spill all. I was going to force her to do a search. I didn't care how crazy she thought I was.

That night I dreamed of a place that I had not been before. It was in the woods, but not the cabins from the trip. I could smell the cedar walls in my sleep. It was a little wood shack. I was there preparing to give birth. I could not tell who was with me.

"Gaby, I forgot to tell you about the vomiting," I blurted the next afternoon.

"You still think you're pregnant?"

"Yeah, I have been throwing up. In the morning mostly."

"Okay. I think you need to talk to your mom."

"Will you help me do a search on the computer? Maybe there is something that can explain this. I need to know the options before I talk to my mother."

"I'll try," she sighed.

We sat at my desk and Gaby entered things that I would never have thought of. We came up with several things. False pregnancy, a psychological condition that simulates pregnancy including weight gain and vomiting. Clearly, this was Gaby's pick. Then there were hermaphrodites, where there are cases of animals reproducing when they have both sexual parts. Then there was something called partheno-genesis. It means to reproduce by fertilizing one's own eggs, mostly in fish. There was a story of a shark that gave birth after being kept alone in a tank for six years. She fertilized her own eggs. I wanted to know more. Even Gaby was interested in this. But she still thought I was losing it. She wanted me to see a doctor and get this out of my head.

That Friday, as Mrs. Adams and I were baking a German chocolate cake, we pored over magazine articles I had found about gingerbread houses. I decided that the stable would be very simple. Just large and three-sided. We could make log-shaped bricks of gingerbread and stack them. We could display it somewhere and light it. Mrs. Adams was getting into it. Her church friends wanted to help.

"Do you think there will ever be another virgin birth?" I asked quietly.

"Oh . . . I guess it is possible, probably not in my lifetime. But we could sure use another savior."

"Have people claimed to be the new Virgin before?"

"Oh, I'm sure. But people claim a lot of things."

"What do you think a new Jesus would do in our lifetime?"

"Oh, He'd have his work cut out for him, that's for sure."

"But what if He is already here, growing up somewhere?"

"I think that we, who believe, would know that. I don't

think it would happen without us knowing. But maybe God has a plan that we would not know about. Anything is possible. That's why we have to be aware and awake and . . . faithful."

"What if Grace had told you she was chosen? What if she had told you that an angel had come to her and said, 'You will bear the son of God?' Would you have believed her? Can you imagine what Mary's parents thought?"

"I would have listened to Grace. She would not take that lightly. You know, Eve, that Mary was chosen because of her character. She was able to withstand the criticism. God chose her because of her strength."

"Did her parents doubt her?"

"At first."

"And Joseph?"

"The angel spoke to Joseph."

"Oh yeah."

For a long time, we baked, and Mrs. Adams told me about when she was young and it was time for her to be confirmed. All the other little girls were getting their dresses and shoes ready. They were excited about the present they would get and how pretty they would look in their white dresses. But she was just in awe. She would just stare out the window, looking for a sign that she was chosen. She was sure God was watching her every move. The story of Mary was her favorite. She wanted to be like Mary.

"I think about Mary all the time. Just a teenage girl, and then boom, everything changed," I said.

"I can tell. You remind me of me."

"I even have dreams that I am Mary," I said so softly that she had to lean in. I closed my eyes, afraid of her reaction.

"I wanted to be Mary," she said, "when I was just a little girl. I wanted God to choose me."

"I think I would be terrified to be the Virgin though," I said. "No one would believe you. They would take you to a mental hospital and you would never be able to go back to school."

"But you see, Eve, none of that would matter."

"You mean the right person would not be afraid?"

"She would pass through the fear. The fear would fall away to greater things." Greater things. I felt a wave of dizziness. I wanted greater things. Maybe throwing up was not the worst thing if it meant I was chosen for something so big. I had chills. Maybe a baby God was my greater thing. Maybe my life was just beginning.

CHAPTER 10

Told You So

When I was in bed that night, I tried to rise above the fear. I was afraid that it would get out that I thought I was the Virgin. I was afraid that my sophomore class would hear that the crazy naked girl thinks she has had an Immaculate Conception now, and she is pregnant with the new Jesus. I was afraid that maybe I was crazy. Those were my fears. And of course, I was afraid of having a baby. If I really was the Virgin . . . I might be able to get over having a baby if it was meant to heal the world: the climate, the violence, the poverty, the gross inequality. I was not afraid of birth—yet, anyway. I was afraid that I was wrong, and that there was something wrong with me. Even I wasn't sure what I thought was happening to me. I was in love with a ghost that protected me and saved me. I felt His presence all the time. It was an overwhelming love. I felt His arms around me, and I felt Him inside of me, in my womb. This is all that I knew. If I went to explain this to someone, my mom, my friend, Mrs. Adams even, they would be afraid for me. They would get me help and it would all come out. I decided that since what I told Dr. Phillips had to remain confidential, I might start with her.

"I have to tell you something that you cannot repeat. I don't know what your duties are to my parents, but you must help me first," I said.

"I am here to help you, Eve."

"So, you won't tell them?"

"You are a minor and I do have certain duties to them. But for now, let me listen to you. We all just want to help you."

I was no fool. I knew that meant she would tell them, but I had no choice.

"Well, I have never had sex. I have never even kissed a boy," I said, evenly.

"Okay. That's very normal at your age."

"But I have all the signs of pregnancy," I continued.

Dr. Phillips did not change her face. She nodded.

"What are the signs?" she asked.

"No period in nine weeks, sore breasts, nausea."

"Those are all the signs."

"So?"

"Well, if you have not had sexual intercourse, you cannot be pregnant. There are things like false pregnancy. I think you need to see a doctor."

"What will that prove?"

"Well certainly if you are pregnant, you should see a doctor. And if you are not, we need to see what is happening with your body."

"I took a test," I said.

"And?"

"It was negative, I think. But I think it's wrong."

"Why are you so sure you are pregnant when you have not had sexual intercourse, and the test was negative?"

"Because . . . there was a faint line, and I feel pregnant."

"Do you want to be pregnant?"

I looked at her and felt my hands begin to tremble.

"I am fifteen. I am in a high school where I want to be invisible. Already I am known as the naked mountain girl. Of course, I do not want to be pregnant."

"Do you think you might be able to leave school if you are pregnant?"

"Dr. Phillips, you are not helping me. I should never have said anything."

"Eve, I am just here to listen to you, make you consider. I will do whatever I can to help you, but I want you to ask yourself why. Can I set up an appointment with a doctor so you can find out?"

"What will he do?"

"He or she will examine you and give you a blood test."

"What if it doesn't show up on the test?"

"Then you are not pregnant."

I looked down. I didn't say anything.

"Eve? Do you think this is a special pregnancy?"

"What do you mean?"

"Well, do you think you got pregnant in a different way?"

"Do you know what parthenogenesis is?"

She thought. "I believe it has something to do with self-fertilization, eggs that fertilize on their own?"

"There was a shark in 2003. It was kept in a tank alone for six years and then became pregnant. They think it was parthenogenesis, yes, self-fertilization."

She nodded. "How did you hear about that?"

"I looked it up on the internet."

"Did you find anything else?"

"Mmm. Virgin birth and hermaphrodites,"

"Virgin births. Has there been more than one?"

"Not that I know of."

"What do you know of the virgin birth?"

"The usual. The angel Gabriel came to Mary and told her she would bear the son of God. She gave birth in a manger to Jesus. Christmas."

"And Christmas is coming. Your father is Jewish. Do you celebrate Christmas?"

"Yes, in a non-religious way. Presents, the tree, lights."

"Does your father mind?"

"No, he likes it. He doesn't believe that Jesus is the son of God, but he likes the festivities. Same with Mom."

"Do you celebrate Hanukkah?"

"A little. One gift. We light a menorah when we remember. When we were little, we played dreidel."

"What about your mother?"

"Oh, she is less religious than my father. But she likes Christmas. Who doesn't?"

"So, you have not really had any religious training?"

"No. Just what Grace has told me, and her mom."

"And Grace had many religious stories?"

"Mmhmm."

"And her mother as well?"

"Yes."

"How often do you see her now?"

"Usually once a week."

"What do you talk about?"

"Well, you know, we bake. We sometimes talk about Grace, sometimes she talks about the Bible, the stories."

"The Virgin Mary?"

"You think she is brainwashing me."

"Not at all. I am trying to find out why your body is doing these things and what you have been focused on. Have you talked about the virgin birth with Mrs. Adams?"

"Yeah. We've been working on nativity cookies. She tells me about her Bible classes and right now it's the birth of Christ."

"Mary is very revered in the Catholic Church. Is she Catholic?"

"She was raised Catholic, but they changed when she got married. So, what do you think?"

"I think we should talk to your mother and set up a doctor's appointment. And . . . I think that you might feel closer to Grace through her mother and their religion, and maybe this has something to do with it."

"My mother will freak."

"She won't freak. She has been through the teenage years

once already. Believe me, mothers have seen it all."

"But I was the easy one."

"You don't need to be, Eve. Your mother can handle it."

When my mother came into the room, I put my head down and let Dr. Phillips do the talking. She made it sound like the most normal thing in the world that I thought I was pregnant without having sex. She made me say the words to my mother, but she filled in the blanks. My mother looked at me while I spoke, and I said the words quickly,

"I've never had sex, but I have all the symptoms of pregnancy," I said, flatly.

Her face seemed magnified to me, big, like it was right in front of me, even though she was across the room. She was open. That is what I saw. Her eyes were wide and round, her mouth ajar, and her skin was soft and relaxed as I said the words. She looked like she had grown younger. I saw it as open like a hole, a blank book, but someone else might say, stunned. I looked back down, and Dr. Phillips continued. While I was still there, my mother called and made an appointment with her gynecologist.

"Eve and I were discussing the different explanations for pregnancy. Often the body will play tricks and cause a false pregnancy. Then Eve has read about something called parthenogenesis. That is when the body fertilizes its own eggs. Eve has done some research."

My mother nodded, not saying anything. She was in shock.

"We'll know more after the examination. Eve, I'd like to talk to your mother for a minute, can you wait outside?"

I got up.

"I'll tell her," I said. And I turned to my mother, who now looked her age again.

"She thinks I want to be the Virgin Mary," I said. And then I left the room and closed the door behind me.

On the drive home, my mother spoke to me very gently, like you do a very old person or one on the verge. She asked why I hadn't told her earlier of the symptoms. She said it would all be okay. She put her hand on my thigh.

"Are you sure there was nothing more in North Carolina? A boy? When you fell, there was no one with you?"

For a minute I thought she could see right through me. She knew what had happened.

"Mom, I was alone at the pond, remember they found me unconscious?"

"But before you fell? Maybe someone left you because they were scared?"

"Mom, I was alone."

"We'll figure it out tomorrow. Don't worry," she said.

I called Gaby and told her about my appointment. She was excited.

"Your mother must be going nuts. My mother would be on my bed, giving me a host of lectures and explaining the procedure in detail. She would . . ."

"What procedure?"

"The abortion."

"So now you think I am pregnant?"

"Well, I'm just saying what my mother would do."

"I don't think I can have an abortion."

"Cause you're not pregnant?"

"Well, even if I am."

"What?"

"If I am pregnant, it's because of some crazy, supernatural reason, and I cannot go and destroy it before I know why or what."

"So, you're going to have a baby at fifteen . . . in high school? You're going to ruin your future?"

"I don't know. I mean, it doesn't have to ruin it completely."

"But you have a choice."

"I know."

"You're not pregnant."

"You're right. I can't be."

First, Dr. Sanford talked to my mother and me. It was obvious he had been given the situation before seeing me. So once again I was the little mental girl who needed lots of support. He was kind and soft-spoken as he explained how he would give me a blood test and examine me. He would tell me what he was doing as he went. Then, in a nice way, he asked my mother to leave.

"Eve, I am sure it is hard to talk to your mother about this kind of thing. But I am a doctor. I see these things every day. There is nothing I have not seen. Even if you've had sexual intercourse only once, you can get pregnant. Is there anything more you can tell me?"

"I have never even kissed a boy."

"Okay, well let's get a gown on and I'll be back in a few minutes to examine you."

When I was alone on the table, I decided I would lay back and close my eyes and disappear. My mother stayed outside, and a nurse entered with the doctor. He told me he would examine my breasts and he did. He asked if they were tender, and I said yes. He asked me what I did in my spare time. He latched onto the running, and we chatted about routes and his daughter who ran track; all this while he moved to my ankles and he spread my legs gently, and placed my feet in the stirrups. I did as I was told and slid forward and then I closed my eyes and tried to go somewhere else while he poked and pressed on my belly. I had barely a chance to slip away and he was done.

"You can get dressed and we'll talk in my office."

"But am I?"

"Eve, your uterus shows signs . . . and your hymen is torn. Do you know what that means?"

"I haven't had sex."

He nodded. "Ok. Let's talk in the office."

There was a large desk with photos of attractive children with big blue eyes. One was of Dr. Sanford with a girl probably a little older than me. She looked like the kind of girl who was good at everything. When he saw me looking at them, he said,

"That's Lindsey. She's the one who ran track."

"She doesn't anymore?"

"No. She has had a rough year. But she still runs."

I looked back at the photo trying to imagine 'rough.' My mother and I sat opposite him in chairs. He started.

"I told Eve that the examination showed that she feels pregnant, and that her hymen is torn."

I watched my mother.

"This usually means that there has been intercourse."

"But there hasn't been," I said.

"It can be caused by other things, say . . . trauma to the area, a certain kind of fall, or even the use of tampons, but that is rare. It is not so rare to have a torn hymen before intercourse. But the combination of her symptoms is telling."

"You are saying that I am lying."

"No honey," my mother jumped in.

"No, Eve. We are trying to diagnose you and provide some explanations. You have had a difficult year, and the mind can be tricky. There is all of this to consider."

"What about the test?" my mother asked. "Why wasn't the pregnancy test she got positive then?"

"They are not 100 percent reliable. And Eve said there was a faint line. Usually, that means a positive. The blood test is positive, but the levels are not in the normal range. I want to get a sonogram."

Not normal, of course. I am not normal. I closed my eyes.

My mother asked me if she could stay in the room for the sonogram. I shrugged my shoulders.

"I don't see why not."

I was afraid of what I would see, but my mother didn't change that. She was in it now. Not normal. As they prepared the machine, I asked,

"What do you mean by not normal levels?"

"The test measures HCG levels. It gives a plus sign if they are high enough, which indicates pregnancy. Your blood test was positive, but the HCG levels were below the normal range."

"So, maybe I am not pregnant."

"That's why we want to take a look."

The screen was black and gray. They showed us the uterus and how it was black and then, after some hunting, there it was, a pulse, a beating heart. Heart. Or so he said. It did not look like much of anything.

I stayed home from school the next day. My parents kept trying to explain to me that the pregnancy was not as upsetting to them as the fact that I could not explain it, and that worried them. The only explanation I had was that I had had a religious experience in the Black Pearl pond with a God that breathed underwater, even though it wasn't sex, but kind of a holy embrace. The same God slept with me at night and had the hair that Grace had. I didn't think this would satisfy them, though, oddly, it did me. Dr. Phillips asked me to tell her about my dreams. I let on that I sometimes had sexual dreams. I even said that there was this one guy in my dreams. Finally, I said,

"I guess he's the one."

"The one. The man in your dreams," Dr. Phillips calmly responded.

"Well. He might be a spirit, but he's the only one that's ever been near me."

"Did you dream about this man before Grace died?"

"I don't think so. It was after . . . more recently."

"Do you think you could get pregnant from a dream?"

I just looked at her.

"I am not *that* crazy. I don't know why I am here. I need to be seeing a real doctor, a scientist who can explain all of this. You people want ME to explain it, and I have nothing to tell you other than I dream about a guy with long hair, and I have not had sex or even been on a date!"

"Didn't Grace have long hair?"

I rolled my eyes and sighed.

At the dinner table, my parents told me that they would take me to another doctor for the procedure. It was early enough that it could be done without surgery, just pills to stop the growth and then empty the uterus. I didn't speak.

"Eve?"

"They haven't even explained the hormone thing, and you are talking about the procedure."

"Well, we want to make it easiest for you. Earlier is better. We don't want you to have to wait, even if they want to run more tests. This is the least invasive procedure, and time is critical."

"Can I be homeschooled?"

"Eve, all of this will be over. No one has to know."

"I want to wait. I want an explanation."

"Maybe there is not one," my father said, gently.

I called Gaby and got my math homework. I had filled her in. She was excited to be the only one in the know, and she really thought there was a scientific explanation. She, being somewhat like me in the social scene of the high school world, felt a rare egg mutation was more plausible than someone like me having sex. But I could tell that in the back of her mind, there was Taylor Watts and his long eyelashes pulling me aside in the cafeteria. She wanted to believe I was a novelty, a freak of nature, but there was that one little thing.

"My parents want to get the procedure over with," I said.

"I told you."

"I'm not going to do it . . . yet, anyway."

"What are you waiting for?"

"An explanation. No one is touching me until they can tell me why and how this happened."

"So, what if they say there is no explanation? You're pregnant, now deal with it. What are you going to do then?"

"Guess I'll have a baby, or whatever it is."

"Eve! You can't."

"I have never been on a date. I have never been kissed. I certainly haven't had sex, so I can't have an abortion. I believe in choice and I would choose abortion for sure if this happened the normal way. I mean, no baby deserves me as a mom. But this is something else and I have to know what."

"You could give it up for adoption. Babies are really hard to come by."

"Well, yeah, if it turns out to be just a regular baby, then I can give it to a couple that really wants a baby, so everyone wins."

"But that might be really hard, you know, once it's here. What does your psychologist say?"

"She thinks I am trying to fill Grace's void."

"With a baby?"

"A baby and a Jesus boyfriend."

"Whoa. Does she think you are nuts?"

"She doesn't say. She says the mind can play tricks, so yes, that's another way of saying, Eve, YOU ARE NUTS."

CHAPTER 11

A New Normal

The next day was Friday and I wanted to go to school. I was sick of everyone hovering over me. My mother begged me to stay home, but I was determined.

"They can't tell, Mom. I won't embarrass you."

"Eve, I am not worried about me."

"It's just another school day. I have a math test. I'm going."

"Well, come home right after school."

"It's baking day."

"Oh no. Skip it just this once."

"No way. We're working on the gingerbread house. She's expecting me."

"Eve, I don't want you around Mrs. Adams today. We have to figure out what we are doing, and I want you home after school. The doctor is calling us."

"Well, I'll check in before I go over. I need to work on the gingerbread. Besides, it's me who has to figure it out. Me. Not we."

"Eve."

"I'll see you after school."

I rode my bike to school. We lived within walking distance and sometimes I rode and sometimes I walked. But today I was late. It was getting really cold. I was hit in the face with a blast that woke me up and startled me in a way my mother had not. I was pregnant. I was fifteen. I was a virgin. That was that.

I locked my bike and sprinted into the warm halls just before the bell rang. Our school was one of the old ones, beautiful in its yellowy gray stone. The ceilings were high and the windows tall and narrow. Echoes filled the halls when you were one of the last to leave. We were said to be lucky to have it instead of one of the low slung, sprawling new high schools that had been erected to fill the growing need for more students. Today I felt lucky to be there. It was warm and I was lost in the sea of loud and clumsy teenagers, just another one of them, not miraculous. When I took my seat in one of the back rows, no one looked my way. I had resumed my nothing status. Though to me the day was completely different than any other I'd had in school. I was different now. I would miss school if I were forced to leave. Gaby was shocked to see me. She shook her head and convinced me to eat lunch with her in the cafeteria.

"I like this school. I don't want to have to leave."

"Well, maybe you won't show until the end. Maybe you can make it. When is it due?"

"End of June."

"Maybe you can get mono at the end of the year or

something."

"Is that what people do?"

"I've heard of that. In books and movies."

"But everyone knows the truth eventually."

"Yeah, but somehow it makes it easier to come back the next year and start over, especially if they haven't seen the evidence."

"Evidence?"

"Eve, I think you should just consider getting it over with. You know, just as your friend, I hope you will think about it. It's your whole life."

I thought about it during English Lit. We were reading *Beowulf*, and I drifted off with no loss. I thought about taking a pill and going home. I thought about going in and getting anesthesia to make me sleep and make me forget. I thought about waking up in a white room and eating soup and Jell-O like I had when I had my tonsils out. I thought about the leaking blood afterward. Then I thought about being free. My parents looking the other way once in a while, my high school life gently flowing from *Beowulf* to Hemingway, from precalculus to calculus and then college. I thought about Taylor Watts and going on a date and being able to drive. Then I thought about the procedure, and Grace's face came to me, soft and pleading, trusting I would do the right thing. The right thing was to go on. To let it happen, see what this was, maybe a blessing and a phenomenon for good, and then decide. Grace would not submit to what everyone thought was the right thing. I had to be strong.

When I got to my house and dropped my backpack on the kitchen floor, my mother was there with bread and fruit and hummus on a plate. She had not had a snack prepared for me since I was ten. This was to keep me home. I sat next to her and ate a piece of bread with hummus.

"Dr. Sanford called."

"Well?"

She shook her head.

"He says the hormone level is not explainable. It is something they see in some forms of cancer, and they wanted to rule that out. But you were negative for cancer."

"Well, I guess that is good."

"Yes, so you are pregnant, Eve. And how is not as important as what now. So, we need to make a decision and make an appointment."

I sighed. "He didn't even want to look into parthenogenesis."

"What?"

"I asked him about it. The egg fertilizing . . . on its own. It has happened before."

"Eve, no matter how it happened, you are pregnant. This is the issue we have to deal with now. I believe you when you say you have never had sex, but you have been sick with grief and trauma. It's possible you may have been raped when you were unconscious. That is the only explanation I can think of. You are still so early, and it is critical to terminate as early as possible. It isn't your fault."

"Mom, I can't have an abortion. I have to know why this happened to *me*."

She began to cry.

I hated this. I was immediately angry with her. She did not have the right to cry, at least in front of me. This was my problem. I knew it would be her problem too, later, but not yet it wasn't.

"Mom, I will go somewhere and have it. You won't have to be part of it."

"Eve, you have no idea. You aren't going anywhere. You are fifteen years old, and you are my daughter, and I will do whatever I have to do. But this is not just your life. You have to think of an innocent baby with a fifteen-year-old mother. In thirteen years, you could have a teenager yourself. It isn't right. It's too hard for you and for the child. You can't give up your future and expect this child to save you. You will cause the suffering of yourself and a little child, and you do not have to. You can make it right."

"I know it's crazy." I softened when I saw her panic rising. "I don't expect it to be easy or fun. But suffering is a little harsh, Mom. I can do better than that."

"Raising a child is not like babysitting. It is 24-7, and a responsibility you cannot imagine. And it's forever."

"This doesn't happen all the time. I have never had sex and I am pregnant. Don't you see? Why can't anyone see that this is different? I can't have an abortion because I don't know what I am aborting. This is not just a pregnancy. It's a miracle."

She shook her head. What could she say to that? She didn't believe me. And time was wasting. Clearly, I was delusional and by the time I could see that, we would have an infant on our hands. That was my mom. She didn't have to say anything more. This was her worst nightmare.

CHAPTER 12

The Manger

"I am going to bake cookies."

"Eve, please don't discuss any of this with Mrs. Adams."

"Duh . . ."

"Well, you know, it just should remain private. I know you like her and trust her, but please wait."

I got up and half nodded. I wanted to talk to Mrs. Adams. So far, no one else had helped me. She believed in the Virgin Mary more than anyone. I knew she would want me to keep the baby, but maybe she would also understand why this was happening to me. The cookies were piling up now. I had the sketch in front of me and we had a near mountain of gingerbread logs. The biggest problem was storing them. We had shellacked them and stacked them in the pantry, but Mrs. Adams barely had room for anything else.

"It's okay. Frank is rarely home for dinner anymore, and Patrick would rather eat pizza and pasta."

"You aren't making pot roast on Wednesday anymore?"

"Sometimes. It was Grace who loved the pot roast."

"I know. She wanted to be a vegetarian, except for your

pot roast. She said she couldn't give it up, even though she told herself it was cow."

"Really?"

"Really."

"It's true. She didn't eat other meat," she said, wrinkling her forehead. "She couldn't stand to think of dead animals."

"Except pot roast," I said smiling.

"Yes, no one else shows up for it. I've thrown out three-quarters of it, so I stopped making it."

"Mrs. Adams, do you believe in reincarnation, I mean in any form?"

"No. It's not in my faith. I believe in Heaven."

"Your people can't come back to you in any form . . . .at all?"

"Well, we will be together in Heaven, but for me, Grace comes to me in my dreams."

"She does?"

"Oh, of course. Sometimes she is a baby, or about four years old. Sometimes she seems older than she was."

"I see her too, in my dreams."

"It's nice, isn't it?"

"Mmmhmm. But sometimes I'm confused."

"Why?"

"Sometimes I think it's Grace, but it's a boy. A boy . . . or a man that looks like her."

"Oh, I think I've had something similar. Sometimes I think she's my mother, and then I realize, oh it's Grace."

"But I think this man wants something from me or wants

to give me something. Or maybe Grace wants something."

"Are they bad dreams?"

"No, oh no. But he comes back and . . . I don't know. He has Grace's face kind of . . . and her hair."

"Do you think Grace is trying to comfort you?"

"It's something else."

"Does it bother you?"

"No. I just want to know what it means. He is always there, and when I was in North Carolina . . . at that pond. I think I saw him in the water, this version of Grace. It's why I fell." I looked away.

"You sound concerned."

"I think something is happening to me."

"Maybe you want something to happen?"

"Like what?"

"Think about what you want most."

"I want to see Grace again, even if it is in my dreams, but this man . . . maybe he isn't Grace at all, and he is always there."

"Eve, do you think you are visited by God?"

"Maybe."

"Is He protecting you? Do you feel safe?"

"I do . . . until I have to talk to the adults. Then . . . then . . . I can't explain myself. They all think I am crazy."

"Oh Evie, you're not crazy. You are grieving."

"I might be crazy though. I had a test, a pregnancy test, and it turns out I am . . . I am pregnant, and I have never done anything with a boy, not even hold hands. Nothing. But

I am pregnant even though it's not possible."

I heard my mother's voice as my words tumbled out, but I could not help it. I had not meant to tell her. Mrs. Adams looked at me and would not let me turn away. She took my face in her hands.

"Eve." She dropped her arms and for a long time she had to catch her breath.

I didn't move except to close my eyes.

"Just like Mary," she said. And she touched my forehead.

"Why me?" I begged.

Mrs. Adams sat down across from me and handed me the prepared dough and a rolling pin. We rolled and cut. Mrs. Adams started talking.

"Mary was chosen because she could bear it. Her character was strong, no matter what was given to her. I always thought Grace had that kind of character. And Grace chose you as her best friend. When we first came to town, Eve, I worried that your family had no faith. I worried that Grace should not be in that environment. But I trusted her. And she was right. She chose the best person. She could not have picked a better friend."

"Do you believe me?"

"I believe you."

"What am I going to do?"

"Trust. Trust in God that it will be okay."

"I'm trying. But my parents . . . they don't want me to have it. My mother is hysterical."

"She is worried for you. You will not have it easy in high

school."

"No kidding. Or at home, apparently."

"Eve, are you sure you are pregnant?"

"I went to a doctor. There was something off about the hormones detected, but they saw . . . we saw . . . a heartbeat."

She closed her eyes.

"I remember the first time I saw Patrick's heartbeat. It was so important for me to see his heart . . . beating, showing us he was alive."

"What am I going to do?"

"Your parents want you to end it?"

I nodded.

"And they don't believe you?"

"No, I don't think they do. My mother says it's not the point. It's what we do about it that matters. How we deal with it. And making a baby have a fifteen-year-old mom is cruel. She thinks I was raped in North Carolina. I think I would remember that."

"Oh Eve."

We finished the last of the logs. Each wall had 120 logs, brick-like primitive rectangles that would be stacked to resemble the shack-like stable we have come to know in all the nativity scenes. The roof was still under construction. We were devising a plan to hold the heavy weight of the cookies. Mrs. Adams had gotten into the project. She had baked behind my back, so that we could move on to the construction phase in time to make mistakes. She had a friend who designed jewelry who had offered to make jeweled details, like offerings, and crowns for the Wise Men. We were making a masterpiece.

Our relationship took on another quality after that Friday afternoon. We worked with our hands and were very quiet. Mrs. Adams spoke to me in careful tones and stroked my hair. She encouraged me to take naps while our masterpiece baked in the oven. She watched me for signs. She made me smoothies. I started going every afternoon instead of running. My mother was aghast, yet unable to keep me home where her rising hysteria was making me jittery. My mother called Mrs. Adams, Beth, and told her nicely that I was to come home after school. She must turn me away. Our family was going through a difficult time, and she was sure that Beth would understand. I heard the conversation in my head and knew what she said without hearing her words.

"Of course, I will do as you ask. But Eve needs compassion, and here she feels relaxed enough to sleep and bake cookies. That is all I offer. I hope that you will let her come back soon. We help each other with our grief."

There was nothing said about the pregnancy, or the Virgin. There was nothing said about God or boys. I stopped going to bake, but I stayed in my room and refused to see Dr. Phillips too. I was now sixteen weeks along. My mother spoke to me gently. She said that it was my decision what to do. They would support me. But I did not speak back. I looked straight ahead, and after ten days, she came into my room and announced that I could see Mrs. Adams if I would just talk to them and resume seeing Dr. Phillips. I had won. Dr. Phillips wanted to put me on medication, but I told her I would not take anything while I was pregnant. Then she forced me to make a plan for bringing a child into the world. We all sat down for that one: my mother, my father, Dr. Phillips, and me.

"I'm due in July. School ends in late May. If I am too big in the last month or so, we can tell them I have mono and I can finish the year at home."

"And then what?"

"And then I give birth and we adjust and then in the fall I go back to school and I get a babysitter. I have savings."

"You mean your college money?"

"Well, yes."

"Are you considering not going to college?" my mother asked, her eyes large.

"No, but that's two years away and I have to think of now. And Mrs. Adams will babysit some. And if you don't want me to be too much of a burden, we could live with them. She said she would be happy to have us."

"Oh my God. Eve, that woman is trying to brainwash you. We are your family, and you are not a burden. Can't you see she is trying to take over? Does she tell you, you are some kind of Christian hero? Are they trying to be a part of this so-called Second Coming?" Her eyes flashed.

"It's just a backup plan in case this is too much for you. It seems like this is too much," I said.

Dr. Phillips intervened. "Meredith, let's keep working on the plan and hear Eve out. So far, Eve has shown a lot of thought."

She turned and frowned at Dr. Phillips.

"We want you at home, Eve. You should know that," my mother said, before she began to cry.

"The point is . . . I have some options. It could be worse," I said.

"Do you plan on keeping the baby a secret while you attend school next year?" Dr. Phillips continued while Mom wept.

"Probably not. It's not that I don't want anyone to know ever."

"You think it will be easier when there is a baby to show?"

"I think a baby in the background is easier to accept than a fifteen-year-old pregnant girl in high school," I answered firmly.

"You see the baby in the background?" Her question only barely rose at the end, as if it were somewhere between a statement and a question.

"As far as my classmates are concerned, yes."

"What about Gaby?"

"I hope she will still be around. But I don't know for sure."

"Have you talked to her about it?"

"Yes."

"What does she think?"

"She thinks it's pretty weird. She is the one who found parthenogenesis."

"She is a scientist?" Again that slight question-statement. I was thinking about how hard it must be for her to have to choose words, and even punctuation, so carefully, like a floor of eggs, at all times.

"She is very academic. She researches. She questions."

"Eve, do you think this baby is special?"

"Special?"

"Different, maybe?"

"I am pregnant through unknown means. So, of course. I think it may not even be a baby. It's something I need to wait and see."

She blinked. "I see."

"And if it is different . . . or special . . . are you prepared for that?'

"Like if it's deformed?"

"Well, that is one thing that all parents have to prepare for. Or possibly handicapped, or sick, or in your case, famous."

"Famous?"

"In that it was a baby conceived by unknown means, as you say."

"I don't know how to prepare for that. I will just have to wait and see."

"You want to continue to go to school?"

"Yes."

"Well, I think we know what we can expect then, in the immediate future. I think this is progress."

My parents stood up then, not feeling progress. But I felt

there had been a breakthrough. I was in control now. I was having this baby.

Things shifted after that meeting. My mother began to focus on my health, my diet. She prepared things with tofu and spinach and had my vitamins next to a glass of orange juice with calcium in the morning. I was feeling good now. My hair was shiny, and my nails grew for the first time. I really glowed. Even I could see it. I started wearing a down vest everywhere and I found a pair of jeans that had skinny legs but a panel across the top for my thickening belly. My mother bought me two pairs and I wore them every day. I was surprised at all the cool maternity clothes online. But really, I wasn't showing at all. I just needed the panel because my old jeans were getting too tight.

Christmas had come and gone. We had built the nativity and put it on display at the mall. People stood in awe. It had really come out beautiful with all the little jewels and glass beads we had added and real hay and twigs. The baby Jesus was wrapped in rags—Grace's old baby doll, Melissa. Mrs. Adams and I were interviewed for the paper. The attention it brought I was not prepared for, and I was extra careful with my wardrobe and my mid-section. *What had inspired us?* they asked. I let Mrs. Adams do the talking. I mostly said that I was into baking something meaningful for the holiday, something that wasn't about the commercial part of Christmas. I felt that the nativity was just something human that would touch everyone, not necessarily only Christians. I found these words coming out of my mouth quite easily. I said the baking was therapeutic.

The kids at school had almost forgotten that I was the naked waterfall girl. There had been a suicide in the eleventh grade and that had made me a nothing once more. However, the nativity in the news made me a weirdo again. It was like I was begging to be noticed when I wanted nothing more than to disappear. Dr. Phillips spent the majority of our sessions on this subject. What was I doing? Maybe I wanted to be discovered? Maybe I wanted to be the fifteen-year-old pregnant girl after all. I sure was getting myself out there. It was just something I had to do, I said. I had no explanation. Of course, though I refused to admit it in words, I did think I was the modern Virgin Mary. Dr. Phillips asked if I thought I, too, would give birth in a manger, or some such unusual spot. More importantly, she wanted to know, did I have a Joseph?

After Christmas, when the manger came down, and I had stopped dreaming about Mary, I dreamed of my waterfall man again. He came to me and looked me up and down and said, "Eve, what have you done?"

That is all I remember of the dream. His face had a look of scorn that I could not forget. I felt violated by this dream. What had I done? I did not dream of him again. I thought about God in the abstract, and I rarely saw him in any form now. It was just a feeling I carried; the way the faithful must feel all the time. I knew why people found Christianity. I felt completely safe and able to let go, knowing I would be taken care of. Even the fact that I was a pregnant teenager with disapproving parents did not scare me. I felt it would all turn out for the best. God's hands.

Gaby and I remained close as I grew. She was the only one who knew my secret, and she felt special because of it, and protective even. It made our friendship closer. She didn't have other close friends at Bend Hill, really, and she didn't feel the need to, because I was enough to handle. She had to let her parents in on my secret though, and they were spooked. They were scholars who had no room for a pregnant teen in their daughter's promising trajectory, and I am sure that they thought they had come to this small town expecting good old-fashioned values for their kids and they got me, a slutty girl with no future. But Gaby loved the drama she had finally found. She had led such a scholarly life. I was exciting! And I needed her guidance in math and science. We played music together still, and now I needed support as the only pregnant teen she had ever known, and even though she was not sure I was the first case of human parthenogenesis, she was not sure of anything, and that made her even more curious.

All of this led to an interesting relationship. She was constantly taking notes on my bodily changes and asking questions. I was having what the doctor said was a completely normal pregnancy. There was nothing odd or outstanding about it. I was at the halfway point; I had gained nine pounds and I had larger breasts that no one but me noticed under my puffy vest. I could see the changes in my face. I normally had a sharp jaw and chin that was now softer. My one ring was tight, and my belly was round and swollen, but small, rather than flat from my years as a runner. It was the height of winter, and I was not running outside, but we had a treadmill that I used when I wasn't too sleepy. I could read and run at the same time. My mother was all for this, as anything that was the old me to her, was good. My sister had come home for the winter break and was simply stunned by my new situation, and a little scared. She was supposed to be the difficult kid.

Raine and I were five years apart and were nearly only children living in the same house. I was born on the day she entered kindergarten and started her new life. She remembers being the center of the world on her first day of school, as her mother was in the hospital "getting that baby out" as she told the class in circle time. She loves to say that was the end of her days in the spotlight, but she knows she always had it on her, while I was the one in the shadows. Aside from that story in my sister's personal narrative, we had nothing in common. She was loud and boisterous and artsy. She had her own style. She was rearranging her wardrobe and creating outfits when she was four. I was quiet and a reader, and my mother had to pick out my clothes until I was twelve. While I had the cello, Raine was on stage. I ran. Raine also ran to keep thin, but she hated it. She took up yoga when her friends did and has not run since. When my parents told her that I was pregnant, she could not believe it.

"Eve, you can tell me what's going on," she said sitting on

the edge of my bed. Then she whispered, "Come on, who is it?"

When I responded, "Didn't they tell you? That's the whole mystery!! I'm a virgin." She laughed nervously.

"I'm not being funny. I've never had sex, and I am a virgin."

"Geez Eve, I'm worried about you."

"Don't be."

"Well, I'm worried about Mom, too. She looks awful."

"She hates what I have done to her. She thought it was hard being your mother . . . and now this."

"Eve, I'm your sister. Tell me what is going on. I promise I won't tell them."

"You know as much as I do. I turned up pregnant, and no one can figure it out. There are scientific explanations, but everyone wants to believe that I am lying, or I forgot . . . I don't know why. It wouldn't be any more difficult to tell them about my sex life. But they choose to go with what is safe, what they know, which is that sex equals baby. Period."

"And you don't believe that?" Raine gasped.

I sighed. "Of course, I do, but not in this case. I know that I am a virgin. I would know if I had sex. Mom thinks I was raped in North Carolina. I think I would remember that."

"But why have a baby? I mean you could have stopped it, and saved everyone all of this. Why would you do this to yourself?"

"I didn't do it to myself. And I have to wait to find out what it's all about because maybe there is a really good reason. If it's all so terrible for me, then I can do an adoption. Right?"

"I don't think it works that way. But I wish you luck. I always thought you were so accommodating, so go with the flow. You are the last person I would have imagined in this position. I get that I took up all the space in the family, but if you needed more attention, there are better ways, " Raine sighed, shaking her head.

"You just don't get it. You don't get me."

After that, Raine tiptoed around me. She was unusually subdued, as if the house had turned on its axis and she now was on the periphery, and all this made her unbalanced. She was rocked by my predicament and couldn't adjust. She began to take care of my mother, bringing her tea and forcing her to sleep in while she walked the dog. Our whole family was rearranging, creeping around. It was weird. Yet in school, I was just back to being avoided. Even Taylor had dropped me and my puffy vest. He had given up trying to get me to like him. But he still said 'Hi' in the halls. He looked at me a little cock-eyed, like he could tell there was something different. I just kept walking.

After we took the nativity down, tossing each now-soggy piece in the garbage, Mrs. Adams and I had trouble getting inspired to bake. We were no longer satisfied with cakes. We had climbed the mountain. We had become artists, and now simply baking seemed dull. We spent a few weeks sitting at the kitchen table, sipping tea, and looking through cookbooks, talking. Mrs. Adams was not a hysterical person by nature, and my condition was simply natural to her. The whole thing seemed to bring her a calm and peace that had been missing since Grace's death. And that made me calm. She had always been a nurturing mother, the old-fashioned kind, that was waiting at home, not driving her kids to every practice and leg-up activity. Patrick and Grace walked to school and did any extra activities there. The Adamses felt the only extracurricular activity needed was church, and they made it clear to their children that God came first, family second, and then school. They were welcome to take on sports and music as long as it did not interfere. And Beth Adams' place was at home in the kitchen preparing meals for her family and studying the Bible. She was really a throwback, but it worked for them, and as a result, Patrick was a respectful, kind son, though he had his own life apart from his family, while Grace had embraced her mother's ways with gusto. She did not notice or care about peer pressure. There was something so much bigger in her world.

So, when I became her surrogate daughter, Mrs. Adams treated me as she would have Grace, I suppose. I assumed she would have believed Grace, however outlandish an Immaculate Conception today sounded, and maybe even feel honored that she had been chosen for this mission, no matter what the community thought. My mother, on the other hand, thought Mrs. Adams would have gone through the roof if Grace had been pregnant at fifteen, and she blurted it out to me as if I should know better. She said that Mrs. Adams found it quaint that the neighbor child might bring the new savior into the world, but had it been *her* daughter, things would be different. My mother just didn't get it. She could only see the pregnant part, the loss of the life that she had planned for me. She couldn't see another path. Even my dad somehow accepted the situation. He was the type that only worried if he could change things. Once the decision was made that I would keep the baby, he went on with his life. I heard them fighting one night early on.

"Paul, how can you act so calmly? She has lost her mind AND she is having a baby. Can you think of anything worse?" she said.

"I know. I am not calm inside. I am devastated. But I have to show her support, Meredith. She has made this choice, and this is it. We can't change it. I am going to help her get through, and then she will be okay, and we will all be okay. She went through a trauma we can't imagine, and if raising a baby is the worst of it, I can accept that. Yes, there are worse things. Ask Beth and Frank Adams about the worst thing."

But my mother fought it. She could not get over it. Every time she looked at me, I felt her holding back tears. It made me crazy.

"You may think Mrs. Adams is a wacko, religious freak, but she likes me for who I am, not who I was going to become. All you see anymore is your pregnant teenage daughter. You don't even know who I am!"

"Eve, that is just not true. Mrs. Adams is removed from you. She is not your mother. She can hold your hand and bake cookies with you. It is not the same. If you need that relationship, I am glad she makes you feel good, but don't equate her love with mine. She is not your mother."

"Well, I thought a mother was someone who supported you in the worst times and . . ."

"You don't think I support you? You are having a baby, and I have embraced that, and you don't feel supported?"

"You have not embraced it. You had no choice. You are stuck with this situation, and you can't stand it."

"You think I don't know you, Eve. You don't know me. I am not stuck. I am here to be whatever you need. But I am a human, and I have feelings and I am sad about your future, yes. And afraid. I am not as cool and collected as Beth Adams, but I am here, and if there is something you need, you just let me know. But let me tell you this, sometimes I might cry and scream, even. I feel things. Maybe if I had God, I wouldn't care about the future, but I'd rather have a heart and a brain."

"You think you are smarter than Mrs. Adams because she has faith. You think she is uneducated and common just because she believes that there is something more powerful than herself and her own plans. But the real difference between her and you is that she believes ME, daughter or not."

My mother was stunned. She could not speak, and I turned on my heels and went out the door. She could not tell me that she did believe me or that she didn't. She was just left standing there. As I walked around the block in the bitter cold without a coat, I thought about what my mother's reaction would be if I just said, "Oh okay, you got me, I had sex once with Taylor Watts." Would she handle that better? Was the problem more a matter of a baby coming, or the fear that I was mentally ill? I think she would be relieved to know that I was not crazy, but really, having a baby come into our lives was a big problem. That and the idea of a rape was killing her. I wondered if there was a part of her, no matter how small, that wished I *was* the new Virgin, so I could be sane, blameless, and not a victim. I wondered why she didn't at least try to talk to Mrs. Adams about it, to get another perspective. Maybe being the chosen family could be amazing. Of course, it would mean admitting that she might be wrong.

Mrs. Adams took me to see her pastor, a wise, quiet, older man who had completely white hair and was no bigger than a skinny seventh grade girl. He looked like God if you could picture Him in a petite, suited form. He sat behind a wide wooden desk and nodded. He didn't get all excited like I thought he would, this miracle coming from Mrs. Adams. It wasn't like I told him I was carrying the messiah. Mrs. Adams, his most loyal parishioner, explained the facts. He said he had heard of similar cases. I perked up at that part.

"What happened? Has there been more than one Jesus that we just don't know about?"

"Well," he said. "People have reasons to believe they have been chosen; throughout history, that is. Never has there been a Second Coming. The mind is mysterious and complicated. But that is not to say that it will never happen."

So, he doubted us. Mrs. Adams was not deterred.

"I have to believe that there is some connection to Grace in this. It seems too coincidental that Eve is experiencing this so soon after Grace's death. We both feel that Grace is trying to reach us," she said, turning to me.

"In what way?" he asked, politely.

"In this unexpected baby. I can't explain it. It is just something I feel," Mrs. Adams said.

"Her room has been very . . . magnetic," I added. "It feels like it pulls me to it. For a while, I felt her there."

"And not anymore?"

"Well, not so much now."

"Why do you think that is?"

"I don't know. I can sleep better in my own room now."

"Since when?"

"Since I came back from a school trip to North Carolina."

"Why do you think that is?"

"Something happened there."

"Do you want to tell me?"

"I . . . was alone in the dark . . . at a waterfall. I had been pulled there. I found it on the first day of the trip, and then I was pulled back to it before dawn on the last morning. I just had to get there. And when I did, I felt . . . God, I think. I saw Him. I felt Him pull me into the water and surround me. I know it was God. They found me unconscious on the side of the pond. I hit my head. I should have drowned. I don't remember getting out."

Pastor Linton looked at me with gentle eyes.

"I see."

"After that, something changed. I didn't feel Grace in her room anymore, and then He was with me all the time, in my head, in my dreams. And then I was throwing up and I took the test. And the doctor told me I was pregnant, for sure."

"I see. Where is Grace in all this?" he continued.

"Her face . . . when I saw God, he looked like Grace . . . a man though . . . and I don't know how to say it, but I feel her with me, only in the form of God. Like it's part God and part Grace. I know it sounds crazy." Mrs. Adams patted my arm.

"I feel that Grace is part of Eve now. I feel it so strongly, it's like she is here. I feel the way I did when I was pregnant with her, like she is very close," Mrs. Adams finished.

"We are looking for guidance," she said. "We don't know what is happening. But we are both willing to wait for answers."

That was the first time I had heard Mrs. Adams say those things about Grace being a part of me and feeling pregnant with Grace. It scared me a little. My mother would be livid. The pastor said that that was exactly what we should be prepared to do . . . wait. God has many ways of coming to us. We should feel blessed and accept his attention. However, we should not expect anything from this baby.

"This will be a special person just for being born. This baby will be loved, I can see. It should be loved for being God's creation, and that is reason enough."

We walked back to the Adamses' house together, but I said I needed to get back to my house. I felt awkward about Mrs. Adams then, even though I was glad to have someone who believed me. Was it for the right reasons? When I saw the pastor doubt us, I was disappointed. Were we both delusional over Grace and God? Her admission to the little old man made me see her the way my mother saw me—deranged and unwell. I didn't want to abandon Mrs. Adams. But I felt like I needed some space from her. She had said that she felt the way she did when she was carrying Grace, and I was bothered by that. Like it was her baby, or she was taking it over. I don't know why. I wanted to know why I felt creeped out by her now. She was the only one who believed me and yet, I felt like now she was trying to make this her miracle. She seemed to really think I was going to bring Grace back. Maybe she didn't even believe the God part, and she had convinced herself that Grace had chosen to be reborn through me, her best friend. Is that why she was so close to me? That was her reason for offering to take us in. She would be overjoyed to have my baby, her baby Grace, in her home. Maybe she didn't even believe it was a virgin birth. I thought she did not believe in reincarnation. But maybe her grief made her forget her religion on that little detail.

I didn't see Mrs. Adams that Friday. She called to make

sure I was okay, and I told her I was going to Gaby's house. We had a school project to get done.

The funny thing is, I had never even held a baby. I had no younger cousins, and I had not ever once babysat. I wasn't sure I liked babies at all. They weren't as cute as puppies or kittens, and there was the poop and diaper thing, and they cried for no reason. I had to ask myself why I was doing this. But it was like I had no choice—baby or not, I was meant to carry this out. I had no doubt in my mind. I tried to imagine it, what it would look like, and if it were a boy, how I would deal with that thing. It was all too weird. But I started looking at babies, and I decided that I liked them when they were sleeping, or when they were laughing or putting their toes in their mouth. I liked them peeking out of snowsuits or kicking their feet. At least part of the time they had to do these things, so maybe I would be okay as a mother. And a baby would grow up. My mother convinced me I would love the baby when it got here. She said she had never liked babies until she had Raine and then me.

"I really did think she was the most beautiful baby in the hospital. I was sure she was special, and I didn't even mind staying up at night. I just rocked her and looked at her. And then there was you, and I was even more relaxed and able to enjoy it. Something happens when you have a baby. You feel like you didn't know anything about yourself before. You open up. Maybe that's why I'm scared for you . . . and for me. It's so powerful, it's frightening. And really exhausting."

CHAPTER 13

Nesting

W e had our good days and bad, my mother and me. We had come to an understanding, or a truce. We were having a baby and our house was going to change forever. We ignored the topic of conception, and it was left to my discussions in Dr. Phillips's office. I have to admit that I was actually glad to have someone to talk to about it since I was not seeing Mrs. Adams so often. I figured that Dr. Phillips did this for a living, so she was used to psychos. I was a better patient, even, if I truly thought I was carrying God's baby. Imagine that . . . she could tell her husband at dinner that her patient thought she was the Virgin Mary. That had to be a first.

But there were moments when she delved into things about Grace and her room, that for some reason made me uncomfortable, and I didn't let myself go there. What was it about her room, and why had I stopped going there in the middle of the night when only a few months ago, I had not been able to stay away? Now, I never even went into Grace's room. When I visited Mrs. Adams, she always suggested I take a nap there and I declined, saying I wasn't tired anymore. Now it made me a little uncomfortable. I was past all that. But just because I had had the incident at the waterfall, it didn't really explain why Grace's room no longer felt good to me. I think that Grace became a part of me sort of, so I no longer needed to go to her room to find her . . . or God. They were with me always now.

I was very confused, and as the birth grew closer, I was getting panicky. What would I deliver? What was I even expecting? When the baby was handed to me, would I know? Would it just be another newborn, all red and wrinkly and floppy? Would I know if it were God's son or daughter, or Grace in infant form? How would I know any of this? Would anyone else know? Somehow, I thought that the world would wake up and follow a star in some modern fashion. The media would be alerted. The news would spread. My hospital room would be roped off. On the other hand, I imagined nothing happening at all, just me and my parents in my room, looking at a regular baby. While I was trying to convince myself it was a gift from Heaven, the nurses would just see another baby in the nursery, like all the others, except for the fact that it was born to the too-young girl down the hall. The nurses would shake their heads and say, "poor little thing" as they bathed and dressed it. They would whisper behind my back. Then they'd send us home where my mother would do her best to keep us hidden until I was back in school making A's and she and a babysitter paced the halls. I think the best she hoped for was help.

Raine had gone back to school, and we were back to our

old routine. We cleared out the guest room so that it would make a retreat for the person who was up at night. My Mom offered to take some nights, but made it clear I was to be the mother, not her. I was not asking for a nursery. The baby would sleep in a bassinet in my room. We didn't think into the future. This made me rethink my room, though. I had never been one of those poster collectors or the type who wanted black walls. But my room was a serious mix of little girl pinks from my five-year-old self, and the junk that had accumulated over the course of ten years or so. Mostly, I had books and papers and sheet music, the cello, a stand, and my bed, usually rumpled, though made, with a comforter that was chambray—a Ralph Lauren phase of Mom's. I had never wanted a decorated room or a theme of any sort.

But apparently now, my nesting impulses were kicking in. I had looked through magazines even, and found a nature-themed room that was spare and calm that I wanted to copy. I cleared out garbage bags full of junk: papers, old stuffed animals, and a failed attempt at a rock collection in first grade. I got rid of stuffed animals that I had never loved, essays from sixth grade, and art kits half done with runaway beads and glue sticks and shells. I felt pangs at each decision, but when I had filled the bags and looked around, I was left with the most elated feeling. I felt defined, triumphant even, over my new space, my new self. Before I had been no one, my room a holding tank, unedited. Now it was clear what I was going for, and soon this clean, nature-inspired superwoman would be the new me.

This cleanout did wonders for my mother's mood too. I had not seen her so happy since she had the kitchen renovated three years before. She was trying to contain her buoyancy, I could tell, so as not to rattle me and discourage me. She was trying to stay on the periphery of my door, calling out, "Don't lift. I'll take the bags out." She wasn't even on me about breaking things into categories for garbage and donations, she was so happy to get the stuff out of the house, and more importantly, to see me as this responsible, orderly person. I could see by the tears gathering in the corners of her eyes that she loved my choice of décor and was off to gather catalogs and paint samples, which she left on my desk. She asked if I wanted to shop for a few pieces of furniture over the weekend, or a rug. But she was casual, like she wouldn't be disappointed if I chose the things without her help.

In the end, she took Gaby and me to some stores and we picked out a rug and a new dresser. I had decided on a pale gray for the walls. It was more of a creamy off-white with only a hint of gray. It was soothing and soft, not industrial. The picture I had on my desk showed a room with similar walls, lots of white bedding, and a bassinet that looked like a nest, all twiggy and dark brown. I painted pale, fawn-colored words, a poem, which created a border around the top of the room. At the end of the passage, a cream-colored ribbon dropped down and attached to an antique mirror. I had to have a bed, a dresser, a desk and computer and a changing table in addition to those few things. My mother suggested that we ditch the changing table and adjust the top of the dresser instead. She bought me a TV for the wall. "Eve, you are going to need a more suite-like space when the baby comes. You'll be up in the middle of the night a lot. I think if you're old enough to have a baby, you can have a TV in your room."

This was a shock, coming from my mother. She was always saying the reason that kids were screwed up today, and had no values and no attention span, was because of TV, and TV in a child's room was the end of the world. This was her way of saying, you are no longer a child, and this baby is not going to take over the house. I wasn't offended. I felt bad about my parents' role in all this. The least I could do was keep the baby out of their way as much as possible. One day when I came home from school, my old pink rug had been replaced with a soft, seagrass one that I had admired in a catalog—just like the real thing, but soft on knees and toes, the ad had said.

It was the end of winter now, the drizzly gray phase that seemed to linger before the sun finally came out, and the kids at school started testing the edges of the dress code. I was still wearing big sweaters, but my vest seemed to accentuate my belly, so I had given it up. I replaced my backpack with a side-slung bag and pulled it around to my front. I was now in my seventh month and was still not visibly pregnant when dressed in my big shirts. It was March, and we got out of school in May. I thought I could hang in there, but my mother reminded me of the often-huge growth in the last trimester.

Gaby assured me no one was spreading rumors. It wasn't like I was skipping parties or Yearbook Club. That had never been my thing. I was still playing the cello, and running, mostly on the treadmill, and my community service project—bathing animals at the vet once a month—was unaffected. My other friends were mostly people I said a word or two to in class. That was pretty much it. There was an awkward moment when I had to do a group project in Social Studies, and we worked one Sunday afternoon at Jade Quillian's house. There were four of us, and the house was warm with heat, and everyone started stripping their sweaters off. I refused, saying I was comfortable, though sweat was forming at my temples. I was close to vomiting by the time we finished. They pushed me a bit, until I excused myself to go to the bathroom and splashed ice-cold water on my face and wrists and even my chest, before I faced them, and made it through. I felt they were looking at me closely, but I covered, and we got back on track. They were used to thinking of me as the odd girl anyway. At the end of that get-together, something happened to me that I had never experienced. Jade, one of the second-tier popular girls, pulled me aside and said that I should change my clothes a little.

"You're really cute, Eve. If you'd just wear something a little less frumpy, and put some products in your hair. I could show you." I blinked my eyes before I shook my head.

"You know me, Jade. I really don't want to be cute."

"Oh," she said, and I headed out the door.

"But thanks," I yelled.

After that, I was a little paranoid that people were looking at me, and I started running to get to class early so I could be seated before anyone who mattered. All of this was wearing me down. I was tired and sometimes fell asleep in class again. I had so many days where my eyes felt so heavy, I just couldn't keep them open. I started taking a nap after school. I stopped worrying about running. I had scary dreams about dropping the baby, or not being able to find it after I had opened door after door. Then I had weird dreams, like the baby was my mother telling me what to do. Or the one where I was a squirrel storing nuts in my cheeks. But occasionally I would have the most beautiful dream. Once I was flying slowly over our town in summer. The trees were really green, and every street had a red tricycle on it. I landed in a field that was overgrown with ivy and as I walked, flowers burst into bloom with every step I took. Soon I was surrounded by fat full flowers and thick tree trunks and towering leafy branches. In one of the trees was a nest about as high as my eyes. I stood on my toes to reach it, but it was gone. When I looked up, I saw Him in the tree. My black-haired man, though I never saw His actual face. He brought the nest to me and together we removed one creamy egg, and watched it hatch into a white dove that flew away. We were left standing there together. But while I was real, He was transparent and ghost-like.

I told my dreams to Dr. Phillips because now that I was having the baby and I wasn't thinking so much about Grace, I had nothing else to talk about. My parents continued to make me see her and she continued to gently delve into my thoughts about sex and boys. I told her I felt fat, not sexy. But she only laughed. Did I want a boyfriend? Hadn't I ever had a crush? Did I like girls? What actors did I like? What did I think about raising a boy? And so on. When I revealed my dreams about the black-haired boy, she brought up Grace. Did I have feelings for Grace that were different?

"Different?"

"Than you've had with other girls. Closer feelings."

"She was my best friend. I was closer to her than anyone else."

"Did you ever feel something different than friendship? Something more?"

"You mean . . . sexual. No. Never."

"Yet in your dreams, you have felt sexual?"

"I guess so, yes."

"Did you ever dream of the black-haired man before Grace died?"

"No. But this is clearly NOT Grace. It is definitely a boy, or a man."

"And he is more than a man, you say, he is God?"

"I . . . well my idea of God, I guess. He is always the one I dream about. And in the pond, He is the one that was there."

"Do you think he really was there or could it have been a vision of sorts?"

"I felt Him."

"What do you mean?

"I felt Him pull me."

"Pull you?"

"Into the water."

"And then?"

"I saw Him and I felt Him."

"Felt him how?"

"He was surrounding me."

"Inside you?"

"I don't know, sort of."

"Was it pleasant?"

"Yes." I looked away.

"Can you tell me something about it?"

"It was comforting and warm and together we were just one being, and I remember His eyes and His hair and the water rushing around us, and then I don't remember anymore."

"You don't remember where he went?"

"No."

"Do you think you fainted?"

"I was unconscious, isn't that the same?"

"Do you think it's possible there could have been an assault?"

"No, I told you it was all very pleasant."

"Do you think that it is possible you were having consensual sex with someone you met but blocked out because it scared you?"

"No. I've told you. I would remember that. I have not had sex."

She nodded.

"You are sure this was a man, but maybe a spirit or God-like man. Not a real man?"

I blinked. I figured she was trying to trick me here. I didn't say anything.

"Eve?"

"I don't know what to say. He felt both dreamlike and real. And they found me alone and alive. I should have drowned, unconscious in the water, but I didn't. I cannot explain that."

"Why do you think you were unconscious?"

"I hit my head. They could see that."

"Mmm."

"Dr. Phillips, can I ask you a question?"

"That's why we're here. Anything."

"What is it that you and my parents really think has happened to me? Be honest."

"Well, we can only guess. The most likely case is that you had a sexual encounter that was traumatic, that you blocked out."

"At the waterfall?"

"Well, given your state then and the timing of the pregnancy . . . yes. You were undressed, you had a concussion, and you say there was a man with you in the pond, who pulled you into the pond. So that is what I imagine happened."

"You and my mother and father."

"Yes."

"Why haven't all of you urged me to find this man, this . . . rapist, in North Carolina?"

"You have maintained that you were not raped, and they examined you and said there was no physical evidence of an assault. I told them it wouldn't help you to focus on that. It is very upsetting to go through that, and, mostly, you have never agreed that that was what happened. We would need you to believe that. Would you like to pursue finding him?"

"Not really. No."

"Why do you think that is?"

"Because I don't think I was raped."

"There's your answer."

"But you do."

"I am not sure. But it is my best guess that you had a sexual encounter there."

"Do you feel sorry for me?"

"Well, I feel empathy towards you. It is hard enough being in high school. I wouldn't wish those days on anyone, and being pregnant at fifteen, makes me concerned for you. I worry for the days ahead. It will be hard. I worry for your future. It has already changed. It will all be harder for you, and life is hard enough. You should have a boyfriend, get older, and then a partner and then a baby. Sorry, I'm old fashioned. And I wonder if you will remember more later, and that will be another struggle."

"But I'm different. I always have been. I never felt I would follow the normal path. I don't feel so bad for me. I never want to go to parties or be a cheerleader. I don't want to stay out all night and drive fast. I like to read and run and play the cello. A baby can't be all that bad for a homebody like me."

"Not bad. Wonderful. I just wish it were later in your life."

"Has no one even bothered to look into parthenogenesis or test me for other abnormalities? Does anyone care about that?"

"Eve, do you think that is why you are pregnant?"

I paused. "Well maybe. It's a better theory than rape in my opinion."

"But is that what you think made you pregnant?"

"Not really."

"Okay, then what is your guess?"

"Well . . . I think I was . . . given . . . a gift. I was chosen as the receiver of life . . . and the father is . . . well . . . a spiritual . . . soul who chose me to carry this child for a reason we don't yet know."

"Why do you think you were chosen?"

"I don't know for sure. But it has something to do with Grace. I feel it. Maybe it is her connection with God now that she is in Heaven. Maybe she chose me."

"Do you think the father of your child . . . is God?"

I breathed in. Then I breathed out. "I am not sure, but it is something spiritual. I don't know if God is one thing. Maybe it's many things."

"What is spiritual?"

"Not human exactly. Of God."

"Like an angel, maybe?"

"That I don't know. 'Of God' is what I feel. In a way that is superhuman."

"Mmmm."

"Dr. Phillips, why is it that we expect *most* people on the earth to have faith or religion? Especially anyone running for office. We expect them to believe in God, and if they don't, people say they are un-American, or too liberal or something, but when I say that I felt God, everyone thinks I am crazy?"

"Well, it is your position that you have had a conception or sex with God."

"That is not what I said."

"It's not?"

"NO!"

"Okay, correct me. What happened in the pond when you were pulled in and you felt him surround you and it was pleasant?"

"I . . . I . . . don't . . . I was . . . given . . . it was a moment of *creation* . . . not sex."

"Okay. Can you remember anything else about what it felt like?

"It was more about being pulled there and comforted. I had to go. I was physically drawn up the hill, into the woods and then into the pond. And I felt warm and happy, embraced."

"Okay."

When I left, I realized I had finally admitted what she was looking for—that I thought I had been chosen to be the modern Virgin because I had an encounter with God that caused a pregnancy. But I had nothing to lose by now. I didn't think they would take the baby away as long as I was with my parents. They wouldn't commit me. My parents would make me keep going to therapy, which I had grown to like. They would try to keep my thoughts a secret more than I would. And maybe there would come a time when I saw that this was just a baby and maybe they were right, that I'd had a "traumatic encounter." Maybe I would remember it and tell them one day. That was no stranger than me being the bride of God, or the baby being Grace reborn for Mrs. Adams. We all had our wacky ideas. I was not the only one.

Mrs. Adams was clearly saddened by our diminishing baking sessions. I still went over, but not every week. I was tired and less interested in baking and she made me nervous, even though she could not have been more interested in me or kinder. I just had the feeling that she was looking through me to the child I would have. She called it "she" even though I did not want to know the sex. She was sure it was a girl. She showed me pictures of her babies, and she wanted to know if I wanted her to fix up their old bassinet. When she insisted on showing it to me, I was shocked to find that it looked remarkably like the one I had seen in the magazine picture of my "nest" room. It was dark brown sculpted iron of woven branches that hung from an arched pole and had a padded basket fitted inside. It took my breath away.

I felt faint and sat down to put my head between my legs before I passed out.

"A Coke, can I have some Coke?" I gasped.

Mrs. Adams ran for the kitchen and returned with a cold Coke on ice, and I lifted my head to sip. I felt immediate relief.

I had been through this before. Even before I was ever pregnant, I was a fainter. I knew that bubbly cold Coke did the trick if you got it in time. When I recovered, I told Mrs. Adams about the picture I had torn out and decorated my room around. I never expected to find a bassinet to match. And it was so unlike Mrs. Adams, so uncute.

"I wondered if you would think it was weird. I sure did when it was given to us. But we were so broke, and it was a family member's work. I tried to focus on the sweet part, it being a nest, you know, and I was able to dress it up with fabric. Both Patrick and Grace were such good sleepers early on, I thought it might bring you luck."

"I love it, just the way it is. It's the coolest thing I've ever seen. Are you sure you want me to have it?"

"Oh, I'm sure."

"Well, when the baby gets bigger, I'll give it back. It will make my room perfectly complete."

"I'm so happy you like it. I have kept it all these years."

Even my mother had to admit it was the perfect addition to my changing room. She didn't like that it came from Mrs. Adams, but the fact that it was Grace's first bed made it okay.

Since I thought I was carrying the holy child, or an angel, or something, my mother was carefully watching me and who I was revealing my story to. One day she asked me outright. "What have you told Gaby?" I said I told her the truth, that I had no idea how I had become pregnant, and her being such a researcher, she was sure there was a cause. She continued to look for things. She figured this happened more often than we knew, that people were reluctant to talk about it.

"And what about Mrs. Adams?" my mom asked.

"She has her own ideas," I said.

"What do you mean?"

"She thinks Grace is somehow coming back through me."

"What?"

"She does."

"She told you that?"

"Sort of."

"She really believes that?"

"I think so."

"Eve, that is scary!"

I shrugged.

"She could be dangerous. Has she asked you to move in again?"

"No, but she says I'm always welcome."

"Well, no wonder she gave you the bassinet."

"Maybe it's just symbolic . . . I mean what she thinks about the baby. Maybe she doesn't really believe it is Grace per se, but life, you know, continuing," I said, trying to ease my mother's fears.

She didn't need this on top of everything else. I didn't fear Mrs. Adams. But I did think she was certain that Grace was coming back to us. I think if she was just able to see the baby once a week, on Fridays, she would have something to live for. We had discussed continuing with baking Fridays, as they were now known. I had all but promised to come over and bring the baby and measure out flour and eggs while she fussed over it. Of course, who knew what I would feel like then. I might be too tired. I might be tempted to leave the baby with her and take a nap in Grace's bed again. Now my mother would have a hairy fit if I let her near the baby.

"I think it's something to be careful of. She lost a child. There is no telling what she is capable of. Grief will change you."

"She's not like that. She just wants to know the baby. She doesn't want to take it."

"We don't know anything for certain. The baby isn't here. And if she told you something as strange as that . . . we should be careful. I thought Catholics did not believe in reincarnation."

"They don't, but Mom, she wants something to hold, I think. She just wants to have a new baby around to remind her of Grace and life going forward and being . . . worth living."

My mother raised her eyebrows.

(Mrs. Adams)

My first good memory is of receiving communion when I was just a wild little girl. My parents were Catholic. I was usually running around in rags, but that day I wore a crisp white dress with a flared slip underneath and white shiny patent leather Mary Janes that I thought were magical. I had ink-black hair and I remember being amazed that I was allowed to stick out my tongue at the priest. I had joy in my heart when I attended church as a child. This is why I have continued the strong faith that I had as a child up until now. I did not have a happy home when I was small, but church three times a week was always warm and full of music and candles and cookies. I knew God was watching over me, and Jesus was my friend. I wanted my own children to have that feeling that I had always had, and know that no matter what, everything would turn out okay, as long as you believed. When I met Frank, who was Methodist, we became part of another church that suited us better in our community.

When Grace was born, I knew I would name her either Faith or Grace. Somehow, she seemed more like a Grace, with the same wet black eyes of both her brother and me. My husband is fair, and if she had had his blue eyes, I might have gone with Faith. But Grace was the right name for her. She was full of grace from day one. She was a quiet baby who smiled shyly and used her fingers delicately. She was careful and deliberate. When she was taken from us, I was sure that she was just too good for this earth. She was God's angel. She always had been. I just wish she hadn't died in the way she did, and at my hands.

I am still struggling to understand why He would do that to us. I know there is an answer, and it can only be that He called her home. I wasn't speeding, but the roads were terrible, and I hadn't replaced my tires when I should have. I had a migraine and Patrick wanted to drive, but I said no. I wasn't at my best. I could barely see the road, but I was sure I could make it home. The other car veered, and I swerved. He had seen a raccoon about to dart out, and when I jerked the car, it began to spin and I had not been focused enough on the river, how close it was, and how deep. I would have guessed we could stand in it that close to the bank, but it dropped right off, fourteen feet, and it was running fast. I prayed that Patrick and Grace would get out. I prayed while locked in my seat and then struggling to swim. I was up above looking down, and still, I could not save her, and poor Patrick, he tried, even in a state of shock. He got me out. He got me out first and went back for her. I hate that. He dove and dove and would not give up. That is what they told me. Patrick doesn't remember or says he does not remember. He will not look at me. He is not the sweet, amiable boy he was just last year, so handsome and easy-going. Now his eyes are narrowed when he looks at me, which is almost never. He eats as fast as he can and leaves the table to do "homework," but his grades do not show that. I want him to talk to me, but he bristles at my presence.

It is Eve that has saved me. She is the only one who will talk with me about Grace. My husband thinks about her. But he tries to fill his mind with work instead of the absence of his baby girl. It is too much for him to think about her, the fact that she will never sit at our table again, never walk down the aisle, never see the Grand Canyon. He has to fill the space that was Grace. Patrick does the same, although he does it physically. He needs to run and lift weights and play ball games. He needs to toss a ball into the air at all times or kick it hard. It is hard for him to sit, even to eat a meal, but I insist on dinner almost every night. He keeps moving. He eats like four people to keep his engine running, and still, he is thinner than he ever was. His grades have suffered so much that Frank and I have told him he will have to give up lacrosse if he does not get them up. He scowls. He hates us. But I know that it is the hate of a little boy, not getting what he wants, and it will pass. I will be there for him when it does. It is a terrible thing that when I lost Grace, I lost Patrick too. The doctor put him on medication after the accident, but now he is off of it, and I wonder how he sleeps. Does he crash and sleep soundly, sunk into deep nothingness? Or does he dream wild dreams, sad ones, scary ones that wake him with his heart pounding? Or does he lie there waiting for the light to come?

I do. A little of each. But I can get back to sleep thinking of her, all the good things about her, the things we did. Grace learning to walk, so serious, so deliberate, and careful, nothing like Patrick, who ran and fell and ran and fell until one day, he could make it across the room without falling. Grace's first day of kindergarten, I remember like it was yesterday. Some of the kids were waving goodbye to their mothers, all eager to get on with the day. Others were wailing, stuck to Mommy's leg. But Grace sat at her table with her hands folded. She could not wave to me, or even say goodbye. She smiled a little smile and held back tears. She slowly lifted the blue crayon from the new box and wrote her name in perfect letters at the top of the paper in front of her. I told her I loved her, and I'd see her soon, and I left as Mrs. Jeeter had instructed. When I picked her up, she gave me a big grin and took my hand. Grace was like that, stoic, eager to please, but as she grew, she had convictions. I never worried about peer pressure with her. She knew who she was, what she believed in. She was not like the other girls in her class.

Eve, of course, was the only one she really spent any time with. The other girls were interested only in boys and makeup and parties. Grace was beautiful without makeup, feminine, lithe. Her posture was impeccable, like a dancer, even though she had given up ballet at eight. I know the boys looked at her. But she had that no-nonsense look about her. She did not know how to flirt, and she let her beliefs be known in a subtle way, her oath to virginity until marriage, and her scorn of drinking and drugs. She was just not a typical adolescent girl, and she was taken away too soon to become what she was meant to be.

I think that is what saddens me the most. Here on earth, here in Bend Hill, we need more girls like Grace. She set an example. She should have been allowed to grow up. I do have anger about that. I do. I ask God why. Why? Why? That is my prayer. Why? And I will wait my whole life if I must for the answer. Because I know there is an answer. Maybe she is getting Heaven ready for me to join her.

I wish Patrick would ask me why so I could let him know that she and Jesus are waiting for us. I want him to feel the comfort I feel. And I try to talk to him. But he turns away. I've begged him to talk to the junior counselor at church. But he is angry and busy, and he keeps running. He thinks I am just old and crazy. So, I am here for him when he is ready. One day he will come to me. I will wait for that too.

Meanwhile, I talk to Eve. As the baby grows, she turns more and more away from me too. If she only knew how wonderful this miracle will turn out. Right now, she thinks she is just a girl in a difficult situation trying to endure, just like Mary. But we are in the presence of something bigger, this baby is determined to be here for a reason. Again, we wait. I wait. I know that in this pain, we have to look for the glimmers of beauty and hope. The baby is hope. It gives me a reason to live. It would make sense for God to take Grace and send a new baby for us to heal. That can be the only explanation. Because God is good.

Eve questions my Christian desire to encourage as many people as I can to accept Jesus as their savior. I do not wish to force my beliefs on anyone because they are mine. I want to share the overwhelming warmth and comfort that comes with the belief in God and Jesus Christ. I want it for every living soul. That is all. The belief in life everlasting. The freedom from worry, knowing that God will provide. I hope to give this one gift to Eve. She deserves this peace. She will make up her own mind, but I am honored to share my knowledge with her when she asks.

When she told me she was pregnant, I understood. I was not in shock or disgusted, even though she was only fifteen, and, of course, unmarried. She went on to tell me the story of her Immaculate Conception, and it was acceptable to me because I had a feeling in my bones that it was a miracle. I feel the love of Grace somewhere in this. I spoke to God and asked for guidance. Every baby arrives for a reason. Was Eve chosen? Was Grace coming to us through Eve in some way? Would this child be a gift from God, not to replace her but to make up for his taking her too soon? Was I expected to support Eve and show her the way? The answers all pointed to yes. Grace would be with me always through Eve. This young girl needs hope and guidance. She just needs God. I am a part of her life for a reason. And she is a part of mine.

I knew that she was coming to our house in the middle of the night. I was taking sedatives and was sleeping deeply because of them, but one night, I got up. I heard something and I went to check. I can see into Grace's room from a certain part of the hall, and I saw a girl seated on her bed. I gasped and panicked. I was struck still, couldn't move. My heart pounded. I thought it was Grace, a sort of ghost. She had come back to her room. But then I thought it might be a robber, and I didn't know what to do. Then I saw her hair. I saw the halo of curls move, and I knew it was Eve. I could see in without her seeing me, and I watched for a while. She touched the pillow and put her hands on the quilt. She pulled her knees to her chest. She put her forehead to her knees, and she sat for a while. Then she got up and she slowly pulled back the quilt. She looked like she was trying not to disturb the sheets. And she got under the covers and was very still. I quietly backed away and went back to my room on the other side of the house. When I checked in the morning, there was no sign Eve had been there. The bed was perfect. The window looked the same. Even the smell was the same, Ivory soap. I wondered if my mind was playing tricks. But I thought I heard the muffled sound of the window sliding up on other nights. I would look at the clock and see that it was usually around the same time . . . 2:30 to 3:00. When I got up at 7:30, the room was always untouched. I took comfort in her being there. I never mentioned it, except that when she came on Fridays and sometimes took a nap in Grace's room, I told her she was welcome there anytime. She seemed to be exhausted from the grief. She had begun to run her troubles away, and she was tired from those many miles on the road. When she came to our home, she was able to relax. And sleep, I guess. I was happy that she got that from our home, and I told her mother so.

Patrick had been a light sleeper off and on in his life, even as a baby. Since the accident, I had tried to talk to him about his sleep. His eyes were often glazed and underlined in purple bags. He said he didn't need sleep, he got enough, some nights better than others. I wondered if he ever heard the window and got up to see, or if he lay frightened in his bed. I wanted to tell him, but something stopped me. After the accident, he refused to even look at Grace's room, as if it had a stench or emitted poison. He locked the bathroom door to her room to make sure it stayed shut. Patrick had been to see a counselor. But he was not ready to talk very much about the accident. He would go when we insisted, but the doctor said he mostly refused to speak. So, we took him to our minister's house to play basketball, and there he said the things we worried about. He couldn't forgive himself. He wished he had died instead of her. He would feel much better if he knew that she had not suffered. He was looking for someone to tell him she had been unconscious and had not been aware of dying. No one did that, so he kept moving while I kept praying and Eve kept questioning.

After Eve went to North Carolina, something changed. She did not come to Grace's room at night. I started waking up to check, but I never heard the sounds again. I made sure the window was open for her. I think that Eve and I became real friends, stirring and sifting and licking spoons on Friday afternoons. She took naps and the house smelled of goodness and butter. She listened to all my stories and Bible study lessons with actual interest, but when she decided to defy her parents and keep the baby, she felt even more like a daughter. It was a dream come true for me. As much as I missed Grace and mourned her loss every day, I was held up by Eve. Then we started our manger project and I saw her even more. I began to believe she was mine. I knew she would go home every day, but while she was there, I could pretend she was my own. It didn't hurt anyone.

When we finished the project and Christmas came and

went, there was a big letdown. We had been so enthusiastic about Christmas and the story of Mary and the baby Jesus. The nativity had been so successful. We were even on television. But really, it was about us being together so much and Eve needing me. After Christmas, after they took our soggy, gingerbread manger down, things changed. Eve still came on Fridays, but her heart wasn't in it. I tried to come up with a Valentine's Day project, but she said she had too much schoolwork and she was tired. It was the dead of winter, of course, and it was depressing, gray every day for weeks. Patrick lived in the gym. I was alone. I went to church more and more often, volunteered in the nursery. Those precious little babies were all that kept me from losing my mind. And Fridays.

Eve was still keeping her pregnancy a secret. No one knew but her family and me. They did not want me to know. I had to assure Meredith London that I was not trying to sway Eve or take over. I told her I just enjoyed her company, and it was everything to me since Grace's death. I did tell her that if Eve did not want to come over anymore, to let her know I would understand, but that her visits were the highlight of my week. I tried to speak to her as a mother. She felt sorry for me, in more ways than one. She couldn't imagine losing her daughter, of course, but also, she thought she was better than me. She thought I was just an uneducated, loony Bible thumper. She is an atheist, so I pray for her. I can't imagine how she gets through the days. But she has not had a real tragedy. That's why this pregnancy has rattled her so. She thinks this is a tragedy.

When we spoke, she did ask me if Eve had told me anything about the baby, or the father. She told me that she did not want to break a confidence, but that it was critical that she be told anything that I knew, for Eve's sake. I told her no. Eve did not understand the conception. That is why she talks to me, because I do not tell her that she is wrong . . . or crazy. I just accept her story. And I assure her everything will be okay.

"She thinks there was an Immaculate Conception," Meredith said.

"I know," I said.

"That is her explanation. She thinks she was chosen, and so it is okay that she is having a baby at fifteen. It is out of her hands."

"Well."

"Did you tell her she could be the Virgin Mother?"

"Oh no. I listened to her, and I answered her questions about the story of Mary and Jesus."

"So, you have talked about the virgin birth?"

"Yes. We discuss the Bible whenever she wants to."

"We are not Christians in our family."

"I know that. Eve knows that. She is just curious. She has told me that your family is open to all religions, so if she asks me things about the Bible, I tell her what I know. Eve is very curious. She talked to Grace about God."

"But Grace was a child. If you are trying to influence her . . . I will have to end your visits."

"Meredith, you are her mother. I don't want to influence your daughter. I am just there for her when she needs comfort. And she has been a great source of comfort for me."

I don't know what Meredith said to Eve. She still came over, but not as often. She didn't want to talk about Jesus much anymore. I was so excited about Easter coming and she didn't seem to care. It made me sad. I think that Eve and her mother had finally become very close, and she had accepted the baby. Eve did not need me anymore. No one did.

When I gave her the cradle, it was the first time I saw Eve light up in a long time. She was thrilled, overcome. She could not imagine me, Beth Adams, with something so unusual and artistic in my possession. It was an iron cradle in the shape of a nest hanging from an arched stand. It was something else. My brother's ex-wife is a sculptor. When I was pregnant with Patrick, she was working on large pieces for an upcoming show. She was quite good, even then, and it was her first big show in the city. She had done a full-size tree and some other abstract pieces from nature. She started the nest and decided mid-way that it would make a good cradle. I had no idea this was going on, and when we went to the opening, and I told her I liked the nest cradle best, she told me it was her gift to the baby. I didn't know what to say. I thought it was very well done, and I certainly admired her abilities, but I was kind of appalled by the thought of my soft little firstborn having to sleep in that hard metal contraption. Nevertheless, I smiled and thanked her graciously, and when James, my brother, delivered it to the house, I was thankful that it had been fitted with a thick, custom pad with sides and a soft blanket. I got used to the thing, and we have several pictures of both Patrick and Grace curled up in their nest next to my bed. Frankly, I was glad when the time came for them both to move on to a crib, so I could put the thing in the basement. I'm not so appreciative of that kind of art, but when I tried to think of something to do for Eve, I dusted it off, and hoped that she would like it. I didn't realize how much. She was thrilled. In addition to being the perfect complement to her new room theme, it had been Grace's first bed. Ginny, my sister-in-law, has since divorced my brother and lives in Vancouver doing huge installations for corporate offices mostly. James has since remarried and had children, and I don't think his new wife would appreciate the cradle in their home.

Easter was coming and it was my favorite time of the year. I asked Eve if she had been reading her Bible and got all excited about the verses on the Resurrection. I could not wait to share it with her. But Eve was uninterested.

"This is the best of everything Christian. The reason we are Christians. Do you want to know how it happened?"

"Not really," she said, rather bluntly. "It is too violent and sad for me to hear about right now. I am still thinking about Mary and Gabriel and Joseph. I don't want to offend you in any way, but I felt something inside of me that was connected to Mary and Jesus. Nothing else I have read in the Bible does that for me. I'm sorry."

"You don't need to be sorry."

"I guess I am not really a Christian."

"That does not make you un-Christian."

"Do you think Grace would be disappointed in me?"

"Grace loved you for who you are."

"But she was hoping I would see the light."

I smiled. "There's plenty of time for that," I said.

CHAPTER 14

Easter

When I go to the doctor, it's funny how they treat me like a regular woman having a baby. The nurse is all nice and excited when she hears the heartbeat. They don't shame me or pretend like I am not really there for a pregnancy visit. I guess this is how they are with all the expectant mothers. It's like a secret club. The problem is that I am out of the club most of the time because no one knows I am pregnant, and if they did, the average person would be horrified. It's just the nurse and the doctor who have to be nice about it. It's a done deal. They just want me to deliver a healthy baby at this point. They want me to give the baby up for adoption and make a bad thing good. I know. They talked to me about this in the beginning. I told them I did not think I could give my baby up. I was pretty sure. But I did not tell them that this baby is different. I am carrying it for a reason, and so I cannot possibly give it away. That I keep to myself.

I had an ultrasound. I saw the baby. It looked just like a baby, the nurse said. I still wonder if it might turn out to be something . . . I don't know . . . alien or strange, emitting light from within. But she said it looked normal all around. I saw the chambers of the heart, the spine, the liver, the eye sockets and the fingers and toes. Even though to me it looks strange and foreign, the technician knows what is normal. I don't want to know the sex. I feel funny about even seeing its face. I don't know what I feel.

I do know that I am starting to get uncomfortable. I have indigestion. I wake up to pee. I feel fat and dumpy, and I think people are looking at me. It's nearly the end of the year. I wonder if I should try to make it a little longer, or make up the mono story. I mean really, I could work at home and go out on a good note. I don't want everyone to realize I am pregnant. I really don't. If I come back to school next fall, and everyone knows I had a baby, that I can deal with. But people looking at me while I am fat and awkward, no. It's like how they say you should never let people know the name you have chosen for your baby, because they will react and sway your opinion. But if you announce the name after the baby has it, they just say, "oh" and accept it and then it just is. Like Gwyneth Paltrow naming her baby Apple, which was such a big joke, but now she's just a girl named Apple.

That's how I feel about the pregnancy. After it is done, they can look at me and feel whatever . . . pity . . . horror . . . disgust . . . empathy . . . or nothing. They can wonder and spread rumors about the father. But then it will be done, and I will just be the weird girl whose best friend died and caused her to lose her mind and pass out naked in a waterfall and get pregnant and keep the baby. They can chalk it up to craziness. I don't care. They already think I'm crazy. I am still seeing Dr Phillips. She thinks I am just a girl grieving. That is the good thing about seeing her—she sees much worse, so I seem pretty normal. I think.

When I see myself naked, it is scary. I have big boobs, which I flatten with a jog bra, and this defined stomach now. For a while, I was just thick and doughy looking, but now I have a hard stomach that comes out over my jeans. When I wear a big shirt, it really is amazing how it disappears, but if I get any bigger, forget it. I think I am going to make it until the last four weeks of school, and then give up. My doctor said he would write a note saying I have mono and need to be home for the next several weeks. My mother said she would go to school and get my work. She hates lying though. I know that she will silently cringe as she stands there making up answers to the school secretary about my sudden illness. But then it will be over, and I can stay home and sleep and read and write papers. I can keep up online. I am sure someone has had mono before. I am sure more than one person has even had a baby before, in the history of Bend Hill High. I'd like to know, actually, how many. I'd like to do research on the subject of pregnant teens and the statistics on those who keep the baby and those who abort and those who give the baby up. I'd like to interview them and understand how they decided what to do.

But for me, the bigger issue is the one about where it came from, and in that, I am all alone. Or am I? How could I find out if there are girls who have been through this? If I could find them and talk to them, I can't think of anything I want more. But of course, that is an impossible dream. So, I am left to ponder my fate alone and come up with a name. But even there I feel paralyzed. How do I name a baby like this? Do I wait and hope that the name will be obvious? Do I plan? I am having a hard time.

I like the idea of naming a girl after a writer or an artist or a place. I kind of like Bronte, like Charlotte and Emily, or Tennyson. Boys are much harder. I think of North Carolina. It seems a fitting source. But the pond was named Black Pearl. And the town was Waynesville. I am not naming my kid Wayne or Blackie. So, I think of Grace and what she would have thought was a good name. If it is a girl, I could name her Grace. It would be appropriate. But it rubs me the wrong way, somehow. I think of Grace, and I can't imagine a little baby trying to fill her shoes. I think the baby should have its own name. I think the name should hit me over the head. But my mother said it isn't always like that. She and Dad knew their first child would be Raine. It was clear because it was a family name and they liked it a lot. Boy or girl, it was Raine. But my name was a challenge. They had lists and they argued. They were stuck at Eve and Lily and Calla. My dad liked Calla and Lily. My mom begged for Eve. But of course, Raine had been from her family, so Dad argued it was his turn. Mom fought till the end and her labor was long. When they told her she needed a c-section, she cried, and my dad promised her she could name the baby Eve, born in the evening. But me, I have no one to argue with.

Of course, my mother gives her opinion: she likes Bronte,

not Tennyson; Dashiell, not Elijah. Even Gaby is no help. She thinks I should name the baby Grace if it is a girl and maybe Gray if it is a boy. I might want to use something of the natural world also, to make her mine, a family tradition of sorts. I don't know. I think it should be obvious. When I was four and Raine was nine, we got our cat, Snowball. Now I think that was such a dumb name. I think, why didn't my mother refuse us? I don't want such a huge thing to rest on my shoulders. I am counting on knowing when the baby looks into my eyes. My mother thinks I better have something prepared, at least a short list.

Dr. Phillips finds it hard to believe that I am flying so low under the radar at school. "Eve, you are a beautiful girl. That and your wardrobe changes and the fact that it is getting warmer make it hard for me to believe that no one notices you."

"First of all, I am not beautiful. I am not even in the mix when it comes to beauty in high school. It is crucial that you are thin and have long, stick-straight hair, and perfect skin, and most importantly, the right makeup and clothes. There are enough girls that meet those requirements, so I am way far from pretty or noticeable."

"I don't believe it. I mean, I was in high school once, and I know what you mean about the long-haired Barbies, but no one can miss your face and eyes, and beautiful skin. I would not know you are pregnant if I wasn't looking for it. I am sure someone is looking at you."

"No one even acknowledges me other than to ask me a

question about math or something. My clothes haven't changed much. I still wear jeans and muted colors. The difference is the size of my shirts, but only recently has it been an issue because it is still pretty chilly at 7:30 am."

"But aren't the other girls stripping down later in the day?"

"Oh yeah, but I was never that type anyway. Gaby dresses pretty much like me, and she isn't pregnant."

"You know that most women really bust out in the last two months."

"I know. I want to quit while I'm ahead. I think I will use the mono excuse for the last month of school. I should be able to keep up with only a month lost."

"Easter's coming. How do you feel about it?"

"Why do you ask?"

"You are so interested in Christian holidays. This is the biggest of them all. I assume you have feelings about it."

"Not really. I have a problem with that part."

"What part?"

"Jesus rising from the dead. The violence."

"Ah."

"I can't quite take it in."

"But you can take in His unusual conception?"

"I guess. Yeah, I can. I have a lot of dreams about it. But the death, I have no feelings about. I don't feel connected to it, the violence, the rising. I feel nothing."

"That's interesting. Have you talked to Mrs. Adams about it?"

"I haven't seen her in almost two weeks. She has talked about it before, but I just can't. It's not as compelling for me and I know that to be a Christian, you have to accept that. So maybe I am not."

"Not what?"

"A true Christian."

"Do you want to be?"

"I don't know, not really. I wanted to for Grace. I thought I was chosen, and to be chosen I would have to believe in God and eternal life. Now I am not so sure. I like to pick and choose."

"What are you not sure of?"

"Of what it means that God could create human life and that I was chosen to bear it."

She waited for me as I searched for words.

"I believe there is God and maybe God creates life . . . . all the time, through humans. Maybe my situation is common, and science just doesn't get it. Do you know what I mean?"

"Not really, but if we believe that God, in whatever form, has a hand in life, who's to say it isn't a bigger hand in some conceptions than others. I think there are miracles and exceptions all the time. We miss them, and maybe yours is not so different. And certainly, there is a world of us who can't agree about conception, and life, and what establishes life and when. No one argues that a mother and a father have to be involved, but then they bring in God too, and who is to say where the lines are drawn."

"See? You do get it."

"You are a thinker, Eve. You have even made me think more. You are a smart girl. I hope you don't give up your educational journey. We need more women like you."

"Well, thanks. And I won't."

Something changed after that. Dr. Phillips had a meeting with my parents. I think she assured them I was doing well. I don't know what she told them. I can only guess that whatever she thinks about the origin of my baby, she said that I am just a pregnant teenager, and I can cut back on the therapy. Soon after they met, I switched to only seeing Dr. Phillips once every two weeks. And I started going to childbirth class. That was an eye-opener.

They found a class for me that had two other unmarried girls, albeit older than me, and two young couples—not the norm for our little suburban town. The guys had very long hair and tattoos, one woman was much older than her partner, and the other couple was two gay men with a woman who was having their baby—a surrogate. I couldn't figure out how they got all of us oddballs in one class in a place not fifteen minutes from my house. It turns out they ran an ad for alternative families, and this is who showed up. Dr. Phillips asked me if I would be more comfortable in a class with other single mothers, but I didn't really care, and when I showed up and we introduced ourselves, I was thinking, I'm still the weirdest one. You could see the faces of all the moms and dads to be rapt when I spoke. I am sixteen now, and I tend to look even younger. I did not reveal my age, and I could tell they were dying to know.

My mother went to the first class with me. Then I asked her if Gaby could come. Gaby was thrilled beyond belief that I wanted her at the birth. After that, my mother attended, but Gaby and I did the exercises. She was my birthing partner. I had to pick a focal point. I felt really silly about these things. I let Gaby pick, and she said we should just bring my iPhone and speakers and that could be the focal point. I figured that was a good idea. Everyone else was using a photo. I thought about changing it to a photo I have of Grace up close, smiling out of one side of her mouth. It is my favorite picture of her. Then I thought about asking Mrs. Adams for the little painting on Grace's bedside, just borrowing it. But I didn't want Mrs. Adams to get over-excited about it.

I really feel uncomfortable around her lately. She couldn't keep her hands off my belly, and she is so sure the baby is a girl, and she wants to tell me every baby Grace story she can think of, especially about her delivery. She has a prayer group now. She asked me to come. I can't tell her that I don't even know how I feel about Jesus anymore. I want to feel like Mary. I really do. I read all those parts of the Bible, and I had the dreams, and I felt what maybe she felt. But the rest of the Bible is just that—the rest, the leftovers. I can't share her excitement anymore, and she can tell.

She is trying to bring me back. She took my hands and kissed them last week. She said she knows that I am confused. But it's okay. I will have the answers soon. This baby was going to be the one to give us the answers and I would no longer be confused. I only have to wait. What is she waiting for? I am worried that she might go to Bible group and tell them or something. She has a way of thinking that what she feels is the truth, that no other truth matters. If she believes it, it is so. And that seems selfish to me.

My parents have always taught me that the beauty of the world is the fact that we are all different, and we have different beliefs and that is good. We should respect each other's beliefs. That is America. We do not have to share our beliefs or bring people over to our side. We can agree to disagree. Mrs. Adams comes from a missionary point of view. She feels it is her duty to convert the "blind." I don't know about that. I don't understand how it can be right to go into underdeveloped countries and bring your beliefs and say that it is salvation for them, that your way is better than theirs because they are brown or poor. Who has that right? Isn't that presumptuous, pompous, and morally, just wrong? Isn't that un-Christian? I am all out of sorts on that subject. I can't understand what they are thinking. I mean, maybe if a Jew, a Buddhist, a Muslim, a Christian and a Hare Krishna all went over there together, they could give some seminars and counseling sessions, and then the people could choose what they want to believe, but this other way just feels one-sided and bullish.

So I am having a hard time listening to Mrs. Adams these days. Funny thing, though, she doesn't mind that I bring this up. I have asked her about the missionaries and it being un-

Christian. She smiles and says, "It is only for the good of those people, Evie. They always have a choice. The missionaries don't force them to believe, but they are given an education about Jesus and God and evil and everlasting life. Then they can choose their future. They can choose to live forever in eternal bliss with Jesus or not. Without the missionaries, they would never have the information. And we want the whole world to have the means to save themselves. We can rest when we have spread the word. It's just education."

"But," I say, "what about their own beliefs? It feels a little like bullying if there is only one idea presented and their beliefs are ignored."

"Well, some people are more loose with their beliefs, or . . . some people are looking for guidance. If their beliefs were so strong, they would keep them. And most are grateful for the knowledge."

"Loose? I don't think loose is the right word."

"Well, what I mean is that sometimes they have less defined ideas or they are searching. They have a right to the Christian view, and then they can choose what is right for them."

"Just like I do."

"Exactly. Missionaries just offer the knowledge that Christians have access to. They should have the same knowledge that we do in every country. And the missionaries make it their life's work to spread this knowledge so that others may choose Jesus. If they want."

"But I have the advantage of an education and questioning everything I am told."

"I believe this kind of education, a Christian one, is good enough for many."

"And what if they choose no?"

"That is their choice. We do not force faith."

"Okay. Mrs. Adams?"

"Yes, Eve?"

"Why aren't the Jews and the Muslims over there doing the same thing?"

"Well . . . they certainly could. They just don't believe as strongly in getting the word out as we do. It is one of our driving beliefs that everyone is entitled to know the way to peace and everlasting life. How can that be bad? Evie, God created man to walk the earth and then to come back to him to live in splendor and grace. This way man is saved and has life eternal. Jesus gave us eternal life through Christianity. The Christians have a duty to give this great gift to all humans, at least to educate them and give them a choice."

"So, if I am Jewish like my father, I will burn in Hell?"

"Eve, that is not what I said."

"But that is ultimately what you mean."

"We are trying to save people, not condemn them to Hell. We are offering salvation."

"But my father and mother are going to Hell?"

"I certainly hope not. They have a lifetime to see the light."

I guess if it is all a choice, it is okay that the Christians want to spread their beliefs in hopes of giving the whole world eternal life. I just wish they could accept all the other beliefs as being as valuable as their own and maybe listen a little. And that Hell would be off the table. Why would any religion conjure up Hell? Or at least, can we send the murderers and rapists and child abusers there? Instead of the non-believers.

I believe that when you die, you don't go to any one place, but your soul is freed from its human container and can go anywhere at any time. You are freed from the confines of earth and humanity, and you become part of the big God. You become God because God is the collection of all the good in us. I would rather know that was my afterlife. I only came to this recently when I tried to say out loud what made the most sense to me. I told Mrs. Adams that and she sighed. She needs the old guy with the beard and those pearly gates and gold streets, but she still smiles and hugs me. She will wait for me to see it her way, I guess.

She has knitted caps and blankets for the baby. She will find a way to baptize it, even if it is in her kitchen sink, I'm sure. I don't want to keep the baby away from her. She is a loving person. She raised Grace after all. And she lost Grace. I want her to have hope again, and new life, and love. I really do. But I don't want my baby to ever be told that its views are wrong. That's when I would stop her. I want my kid to be a Buddhist if that's what it wants and have its own ideas without being influenced about a perfect afterlife. Because a little kid would think that was better than being freed into the ether. A little kid would want Heaven because it is simple and definite and they probably promise ice cream there every day too. And then that little kid would grow up and that belief would have been burned into its brain, and there would be no questioning of its merit. I want my kid to question everything. Maybe that is what I was able to offer Grace—the questions, and another perspective. She was pure and strong, and she taught me, but I had something to offer her too.

When I asked Mrs. Adams what Easter means to her, she literally lit up.

"You know, Grace was an Easter baby. She was born the week of Easter. We had a dress all picked out for her, and when I left the hospital, we practically went straight to services with our little pink bundle. I was so happy that Easter. It is always my favorite holiday. The children are so pretty in their dresses and new shiny, patent leather shoes. The air smells like grass, sometimes. After the winter, it feels like we are reborn. I feel lighter and fresh. I am so happy to see my legs and be free of the smell of wool. The flowers poke out of the ground. Dyeing the eggs and hiding them is so joyous. I love the baby birds. And when I pray, I can almost feel the pain He felt. I feel the wounds. I fast so I am closer to Him. I understand what drives my beliefs and my life here on earth. I can't imagine living here a whole lifetime just thinking I am going to clean and cook and take walks and see my children leave, and then in the end, I will die and it will all be over, just me in the ground. I can't imagine the sadness that must bring to an old person, to someone dying of cancer. My goodness, I have more hope than that, more expectation. I live everyday knowing that my life here is what will lead me to God and to Heaven where I will be with Grace. Without that, how could I go on?"

She had a point. No wonder the Christians have no doubt, and live to spread the word. How lucky for them, that they have that comfort and the knowledge that they will join their sons and daughters, and mothers and fathers. But for the rest of us, should we forget our questions, forget our science, forget what we have learned and give it up to faith, a shot in the dark . . . on the chance that they may be right? I just can't force myself to believe something that feels like a fantasy. I am only sixteen. I have a whole life to ponder these things. But right now, I am pregnant for no reason, and I have to indulge Mrs. Adams, and hope that she will be reunited with Grace, and maybe I will too. And if not, we will be together as earth and trees reaching toward the sky. That's not a bad thought either.

When I was little, my dad used to read the story *The Polar Express* with Raine and me every Christmas. I guess it was not so religious, and he was always into the beautiful parts of Christmas anyway. On Christmas Eve, my mom would let us open one gift, and we already knew it was a new flannel Lanz nightgown. Then we made hot chocolate and Dad would read the book in front of the fire. Raine hated it. She was so much older than me and had heard it too many times. She voted that we read the shorter *Night Before Christmas* until she got her wish and he read both, which made her even madder. But *The Polar Express* was one of my father's favorite books. The year I was nine, and I finally realized that Santa was my parents, I asked him what he liked so much about the story. He said he loved the illustrations for one thing, and he loved the idea of the black train barreling through the snow in the night. But the real heart of the story was the boy's faith. The fact that he believed in something he could not see. "I love his passion and faith. He doesn't give up his faith even when everyone else does."

I wanted to remind my dad again about believing in something you cannot see.

"Dad, remember when I asked you why you love *The Polar Express?*"

"Well, yes, I think I do."

"Do you remember what you said?"

"I imagine something like . . . I like the train in the snow. I always loved trains. And I like the boy and the fact that he won't give up his beliefs."

"Yeah, you said that the heart of the story was about a boy who believed in something he cannot see."

"That's right."

"But doesn't science tell us that we need proof?"

"Yes, science does."

"So . . . can I skip chemistry on the basis of faith?"

"No," he smiled. "Science is very important, but there is more to life than science. That doesn't mean you shouldn't learn about it. You're a better person, educating yourself. Then you can make smart decisions about what you believe."

"Do you believe in what you cannot see?"

"Yes, Eve, I do. I believe in peace, and music, and oxygen, and I believe in God."

"Is that why you don't seem so upset over my pregnancy? Is that why you don't grill me like everyone else does?"

He looked at me carefully, solemnly. "I believe you are telling us what you know. I believe in you, Eve."

"Have you told Mom that?"

"Yes, I have."

"Does she think we're nuts?"

"A little."

The last day of school was May 28th. This year Easter was late, April 24th. It made sense that I should skip the last month when I woke up Easter Sunday and it was a sunny glorious spring day, like we hadn't seen since early fall. I stood before my window feeling large and doughy, knowing I could no more put on a cotton dress than I could speak Italian. I took a shower and dressed in a pink striped Oxford shirt and leggings that made my legs look skinny. At least I looked tall. I knew I could not be seen in public again. I joined my parents in the kitchen and told them I wasn't going back to school. I was fat and the weather had turned. I had been able to hide in the gloomy rainy months before, but this day, Easter, was a sign of things to come. I knew that on Monday, the halls would be filled with new t-shirts in bright colors and pastels, sandals, and shorts even. There was no place for maternity clothes, or me. From the look on my mother's face, it was clear she agreed. I would be home, eating and sleeping, fulfilling my requirements for the last month of tenth grade. Mono. Gaby would be my liaison. I was sure that only math would be a problem, and I had all day to work it out.

I was prepared for something big to happen on Easter. It seemed that this is the way it went. If I sat and breathed, if I did not think or plan, I would receive the calm that I needed to go on. On this day, surely, something would come. When we were little, we dyed eggs and my parents hid them in the yard. We took our baskets and emptied them of the chocolate bunny and the jellybeans and the Cadbury Egg and bubbles, and we went out into the grass where I was given a head start and Raine followed. She still always got the most eggs, but one year I got the Golden Egg, and inside was a five-dollar bill. I had been obsessed with money at the time and the thought of five dollars was like the lottery. More than that, I had won the prize for the first time instead of Raine. She acted all cool, but I knew she was steaming. This year she was not here. She had finals coming up and had met a new guy. So, Mom and Dad and I opened the kitchen doors and took our blueberry pancakes and coffee outside.

We talked about the sun and the flowers. A calm had come over us. I was home now. I wasn't going out. We were in for the long haul. The rest of the day was weird. Usually, we went to a state park area and hiked, or saw a movie if it was rainy, or drove to the city for lunch.

But today it was so shockingly sunny, and I was so, all of a sudden, huge, we seemed stunned. My mother finally decided to go to Home Depot, open 364 days a year, and buy plants, and when she returned, the two of us rolled up our sleeves and dug holes under the warm sky. I thought about Mrs. Adams in the front row of the little church on Woods Avenue. I pictured the prayer she would say for Grace, and the dinner the Adams family would have around the dining room table, finally. I imagined the lemon cake she would have made without me. I hadn't seen her in weeks. Two weeks ago, I was much smaller and agile. I could run three miles. Now I could barely balance enough to dig the dirt out of the ground. I was a real pregnant person. Before this day, I had sort of convinced myself that maybe it was all a joke. I had disguised my appearance for the whole school and there was a part of me that believed the costume. Now I knew for sure, there was no turning back. I still had to be a large awkward pregnant person for a whole two months before I would turn from that new animal into a mother. It was hitting me hard.

As I dug on my knees, tears rolled down my face. The day was mocking me. The bright cheeriness made me feel all the more lonely and sad. If it had been dreary, I could have been wrapped up in a movie, under a blanket. On this Easter Sunday, I had to look at my body and get outside in the small cell of my backyard, the picture of things to come. My mother was busy pulling and hauling, so she let me dig quietly, not interrupting my sobs. Then I wiped my eyes and breathed in and out. I looked around the garden and saw how beautiful

it was. My mother had been out here in the drizzle, working
for weeks, and I was just noticing the lushness of the trees,
their apple green, new leaves rustling. I saw the variety of
greens unfurled. My mother was not a pastel person, so she
chose to focus on lots of different leafy plants and some white
flowers. In the focal area, an old stone bench towards the
rear, she had planted deep purple tulips and they were
poking through. Above me was the far away baby blue sky,
reaching all the way to my sister's apartment, to my
grandmother's house in California, and beyond. I was here in
this spot, and lucky to be here. I had these trees to hug, and
the sky if I needed to go somewhere in my dreams. At night,
I had the moon. Our garden was so full, I would have to go
to my room and roll out the window and lean out to see it,
but I could and that is what I needed. When I looked at the
moon, I knew that Gaby could see the same moon, and so
could Mrs. Adams and so could my grandmother. It was
possible that even Grace was looking at the moon. It made
me feel small, which is what I needed. This is what got me
through.

It wasn't as if I was bedridden. Even though I was
supposed to be sick enough to miss a month of school and
finals, my mother smuggled me out and we drove. We drove
and then hiked to keep from going stir crazy. I was doing my
schoolwork and then napping some to make up for the
wakeful nights I had. Then we would drive, and I would walk
off my fear. I was reading baby name books and making lists.
Gabriel? Ella? Bronwyn? Sky? Plum?

The birthing class was almost over, and I only knew that I would want the epidural. Two of the people in our class were adamant about not having drugs of any kind. They were taking yoga classes daily. One of them was having a hypnotist in the birthing room. I said, "bring it on" to the epidural. I didn't want to be a screaming lunatic. I had seen the films. I wasn't glamorizing the birth in any way. Gaby was all excited about watching the baby emerge, but not me. I just wanted it out. She was my partner in crime. She had to tell her parents about me but swore them to secrecy, and they still let her come over and tutor me and make me her project. I never saw them again. I was too embarrassed. They knew all about the North Carolina fall, and now this, and they probably wanted to take her back to Brazil where they may have had guards, but no crazy friends. I don't know what I would have done without Gaby. As we grew closer, I had guilt about replacing Grace. We were now hanging out on my bed and giggling and gossiping about TV shows and classmates, watching YouTube, stuff Grace wouldn't have done. And I was having fun. I didn't want to die anymore.

* * *

I was down to 27 days to the due date. School would be over in three days, and I would have gotten away with my mono excuse. But after I had missed a week in school and my mother had gone to the Vice Principal with the note and the huge task of lying to protect me, and then asking for help to keep up my good standing, I was feeling funny about the lie.

I got handwritten notes from some of my teachers, and a phone call from Mrs. Meeks, my language arts teacher. She was my favorite. My mother told her I was sleeping, but I knew I would have to return the call. My mother and I talked about an alternative to the lies. What if I told them the truth? It was not like I was not going to see these people ever again. I would be back in school in the fall, and I would have to face them, and the fact that I had lied. The kids were one thing. They had their own lives to worry and think about. They would not care, but Mrs. Meeks would wonder why I had not trusted her with my predicament. I would be horribly embarrassed and guilt-ridden. I had considered changing schools. I could start fresh at Henson Hill, the good Episcopal high school in Bentley. It was only a fifteen-minute drive, and they had plenty of non-religious kids there. I could most likely get in with my grades. There was usually a spot in the upper grades as few people transferred then. We had investigated this option. But really, I wanted to finish school at Bend Hill High. I didn't want to be the new kid. So when the call came from Mrs. Meeks, my mother and I decided that I should let her know. I wrote this email:

Dear Mrs. Meeks,

I want to thank you for your concern about my health, and my inability to finish the school year. Actually, I am very tired and uncomfortable, but I do not have mononucleosis. I am pregnant. My family and I have decided that it is the best thing for me to finish my studies at home before the birth of the baby. I felt horrible deceiving you, and I wanted you to know the truth about my situation. I would appreciate it if you would keep this information very private. I will be returning to school in the fall. These are unusual circumstances, but I feel I have made the right decision, and my family is supportive. I will do my best to finish the year with the best effort, and I have plenty of time to read. Thank you again for your concern. I will see you next year.

Warmly,

Eve London

Then my mother asked if she could call Mrs. Meeks back and talk to her. I was okay with that.

"She was so happy to hear from me. She was really worried about you, and honestly, she just could not believe that you are having a baby. I talked to her for a long time. I told her not to get into it with the other teachers; that it was very private, and that we were all fine and moving forward. But I told her about the year you have had, and the odd circumstances you were in. I hope you don't mind. I felt she needed some reassurance."

"It's okay."

"She felt better about everything. I told her you would be continuing school as usual with our help. That helped a lot. I think that for her, it is something so foreign. She is so young and newly married. She sees the world in perfect order, and she said that her parents would have abandoned her in the same situation. I think she was almost envious of our family. She said she wanted to visit you sometime. I told her I would talk to you about it."

"I guess that would be okay, maybe after the baby comes."

"So, it's done. It was the right thing."

"Do you think it will get out?"

"Does it matter now?"

"Only if they want to kick me out of school."

"No, that's the last thing they want."

"Then no, it really doesn't."

I felt a huge weight off my chest, and I immediately went to sleep. For the next three weeks, I worked on the computer and took my finals and aced them—all but precalculus, where I got a B. Then I started reading fiction and watching the scale. I had really been small for the first eight months of the pregnancy, then I had been pregnant looking, now I was downright huge. In the 36th week through the 38th, I put on four pounds, and I'd swear it was all in my feet and belly. I could sit a full-size plate on my stomach. I had gained 21 pounds, all in the front. Everyone said it meant it was a boy. I had limited my exposure to other towns and the park where we hiked, but the few people who saw me said without fail, "Oh now, that's a boy, mark my word!" Baby Jesus was a boy. But this is a new day, and I would think God would come back as a girl anyway.

CHAPTER 15

Birth

A weird thing happened. I finally became attached to the baby in the last month. It was moving all over the place, and we had hours together in the middle of the night where it was just us in bed, me watching the antics of my rolling belly, an actual foot jutting out of my right side. It was really amazing. I finally felt that it was my baby, and we were alone against the world. I sang to it and put my hands on the parts that jutted out. I pushed, and he or she pushed back.

We were communicating. I put my headphones on my belly, and it went crazy, especially over Brandi Carlisle and The National. Even though I couldn't wait to get it out, I was going to miss these nights playing with this silent creature. It was quiet and didn't ask for anything. It was all mine. And I liked the feel of something alive in me. My baby was the only one who knew what I knew. I had more dreams, vivid dreams of Jesus again. He was back, now inside of me in the form of this baby that was not a baby, but a miniature man with long black hair. He would swim and surface and laugh. He would roll around and I would chase Him, but never catch Him, as I was fat and clumsy, and He was fluid and seal-like. Then

He would be all around me, like air, like I had felt in the pond, and I felt like I was drowning, and then I would wake up.

For a while I had lost that religious fervor that had come to me after Grace died. Now I felt the blanket of God over me again, in me, like it was back then in the pond, to the point that I could not separate what was the baby and what was me and what was God. I felt cloaked and separate from the world. I stopped talking and slept, waiting to see him again and again. I cried in my bed, wondering if this was the baby I was seeing and feeling, or its father, or was I just plain going crazy? My parents were worried about me, and discussed my withdrawal with the obstetrician and Dr. Phillips. I was back in her office. For the first time, I let her know what I was going through in the moment.

"I have trouble getting a breath. I am surrounded by this feeling. It's like I am swimming in water that is a person, God, a baby, a man. I don't know what it is. I feel like I am drowning, but I feel so happy . . . so elated. I don't want it to end. I don't want the baby to be born. I want to stay like this. I am happier than I've ever been. I feel the whole world is inside of me and I just have to close my eyes and look."

"Wow," Dr. Phillips said. "That's a lot to feel. No wonder you're exhausted."

"Is this what women feel when they are about to give birth?"

"It varies. Some women want to hold on. Most are ready to get it out. But I think you have other feelings in addition to the birth."

"Because I am so young."

"Is that what you think?"

"That's what is different about me."

"A lot of teenagers get pregnant."

"Not like me."

"Because?"

"There is no father."

"And you arè waiting to see your baby to see if there is an answer . . . but more."

"What?"

"You tell me."

"I want to know if it looks like Him?"

She looked at me and didn't talk.

"I think when the baby is born, it might bring . . . some answers." I said.

"Do you have any idea how?"

"I feel like I will know everything when I see the baby."

"You will know what?"

"If it is different. If it is like Grace, or some part of this God I feel. Or just a baby."

"What will tell you?"

"The baby. And the way others react to it. I am expecting there to be something different."

"And what if it looks like a regular, beautiful baby?"

I shrugged. "Maybe then I can rest, too."

"So, I would think you would be ready for the birth. Ready to know either way so that you can rest."

"But even though I am so tired, I have never been so . . ."

I took a breath. "Euphoric. I think this is what it feels like to be in love. And I am afraid that part will end."

She smiled. "You will be in love with your baby. Some mothers feel it immediately and others take some time, but you will, trust me."

"I hope so," I sighed.

Mrs. Adams called to check on me about twice a week. She wanted to visit. It had been six weeks since I had seen her. Finally, I said okay, she could come over. My mother made some lemonade and she brought cookies, and we sat on the porch, until my mother excused herself for a phone call. Then it was just the two of us. I was wearing a long top and leggings and felt like a cow, and she was in one of her flowy dresses. She was so pretty and young-looking. She was the one who should be a new mom.

"Thank you for letting me see you, Eve. I have missed you so much. Baking isn't the same, and I hardly have a soul to talk to anymore."

"I'm sorry Mrs. Adams. I've just been so tired from exams, and I don't sleep well at night, so I just haven't felt up to guests."

"Oh, please don't think of me as a guest. I only want to bring you some goodies and hear your voice. You don't ever have to bother for me. I'd be happy to watch you sleep."

"Okay," I laughed.

"I just mean that I miss you. I hope I haven't been a bother to you. Have you been baking at all?"

"No. I don't really do that here. I guess it's more fun with you. But I just haven't wanted to get out at all. I guess it's the nesting."

"I remember it well."

"I've cleaned out my room and color-coded my files. We bought all sorts of containers for the bathroom, and my mom and I have spent a lot of time in the garden."

"That's wonderful. That's what you should be doing."

"And sleeping. I take a nap every day. It feels so nice to just sleep whenever you feel sleepy and eat whenever you want. I've become a grilled cheese addict."

"That's better than a brownie addict."

"Yeah. So, I hope when the baby comes, I'll want to move around more. Right now, I am taking advantage of my excuse to be a sloth."

"I am glad to hear that you're so well. I just want to offer myself up. Anything you need . . . or want. Just call me. I have all the time in the world."

"Thank you, Mrs. Adams."

"And it's okay to be scared. Everyone is scared when they have their first baby. So, when you have that pain, just know that it is going to end and you will have the most wonderful gift in the world. A blessing. And Eve, there is one more thing I want to tell you. I know what you are feeling, some of it at least. When I found out I was pregnant with Patrick, I was a teenager, not much older than you. Frank and I were not married. And everything turned out just fine. Great, even."

My jaw literally fell. "Oh."

"Yes, just because I am a good Christian does not mean I am perfect."

"Do they know? Did Grace and Patrick know?"

"No. But I wanted you to know. Everything turned out."

"But Grace was so adamant about saving her heart for marriage. You told her that was so important."

"Yes. That is what we taught her. And I hoped she would. But I am human, Eve. We all are. And we can be forgiven."

She patted me. I nodded.

"I better get going . . . Eve, will you call me when the baby is born? Just let me know . . . I won't bother you if you want some time. I just want to know everyone is okay."

"Of course. We'll call right away. I have no one else to tell."

I watched her walk to the street and her body looked defeated. She was moving slowly and her hands looked like they wanted something to grab. I closed the door and wandered into the kitchen. I preheated the oven and started mixing flour and eggs and melting the chocolate. We hadn't made her special brownies in ages. I was trying to watch my chocolate intake. But I had the sour cream and everything. When they were cooled, I cut them in squares and wrapped them in a dish towel with a ribbon and I asked my Mom to take them over and put them on the step. I knew Mr. Adams would be home soon. My note said:

Mrs. Adams,

I made your recipe from memory. You taught me

everything about baking and being a good friend. I'll never forget your kindness and support during this year.

Love, Eve

It was the final week. I was going to my obstetrician every third day now. I was a high-risk pregnancy because of my age. I hated going. I liked the doctor and the nurse well enough, but that waiting room, God. It was painful, my mother and I sitting there with all the 25- to 40-year-olds beaming and comparing notes. We always seemed engrossed in our own conversation, Mom and me. There was always some serious thing we needed to discuss right then, so no one looked to us for tidbits about the final weeks. When they called my name and I had to heave myself off the chair and waddle across the floor, it seemed like the longest walk of my life. I just felt the eyes of those women on my aching back, and I knew that as soon as the door closed, they were abuzz with questions about that 'poor little girl' and worse, 'her poor mother.'

My mother was holding up. She had really come through for me. She had stopped the crying a long time ago and was always positive and sweet with me. I had seen a change in her that was downright spiritual. She had always been the no-nonsense mom, the cut to the chase, get-down-to-business, non-fluff mom. My mother hadn't been the one to run my homework or lunch to school if I forgot it. She was big on responsibility and letting us learn the hard way. She did not baby us. In the last few months, though, she had brought me food in bed, massaged my feet, helped me clean out my room, let me get away without doing the dishes. I think she was seeing the final days of my childhood coming to a screeching halt, and she wanted me to be a child again—her child, her last one. One day, she came to my room with tea and cookies and a bottle of lotion. She rubbed my feet while I ate. "You will always be *my* baby," she said. She had a new look on her face, not a look I'd seen on her before: beatific, serene, almost like Mrs. Adams.

"You know Oprah was pregnant when she was fourteen," she said to me.

"She was?"

"Mmmhmm."

"What does that mean?"

"Well. I never want you to think your life is over. Look where she is."

"I don't think my life is over. I think my life is just different. Weird. I've never been like everyone else."

"What does that mean?" she wrinkled her brow.

"Mom, I have never fit in. I have always been an outcast. Grace was my only real friend. That's a little unusual."

"What about Gaby?"

"And now Gaby, and Gaby is another outcast. She is an intellectual, geek teenager. Grace was a Jesus freak. These are my friends. We just don't fit in."

"And what are you?"

"Naked waterfall girl. Pregnant virgin. Psycho. Dropout.

Take your pick."

"Eve. Everyone has hard times at some point in their lives. You got help. That is what matters. It doesn't make you a psycho. And you haven't dropped out. Those popular kids will peak at seventeen. You have a bright future. I promise." I thought it was hilarious that she left out the pregnant, virgin part.

"But everyone will think I'm done."

"They will think you have mono. And they are teenagers. They are thinking about their hair and their cars, not you."

"The teachers will think it's over for me."

"I think you are wrong."

"Well."

"You have us. We will help you get back on track. It won't be easy, but we're here."

"I don't expect you to take care of a new baby. I promise."

"I know. But I might like it. When it's a toddler, it's all yours."

"Do you think I can do it?"

"Take care of a baby?"

"Yeah. And love it?"

"Of course."

"I've never even had a boyfriend to love. I never babysat. Why do you think I can do it?"

"Because you chose to do it. And you can do anything."

"Yeah. I chose."

I was in bed that night making an X on the calendar, three

days to go. It was June 15th. I could see the moon out my window. It was high and close to full, but not quite there. My room was ready. It was now a woman's room. My bed was the white iron bed my grandmother had used in her first house. Then it had been my mother's, now it was mine. It rose to an oval ring at the center of the four posts. When she was a girl, my mother had draped pink tulle over the canopy, but my bed was bare. I had a creamy, fat, goose down comforter and Matelassé pillow shams. Next to my bed was my desk, an antique walnut table of sorts with a drawer. Across from my bed was the baby's dresser. It was just the right height to change a diaper. And it was dark wood, almost Shaker in style. Next to it was a tiny child's chair my mom had found in an antique shop, weathered and peeling. Next to my bed was the nest bassinet. It was glorious, and the whole room in its simplicity allowed it to shine. It was the crowning jewel. I loved it so much. I was afraid Mrs. Adams would change her mind and take it back. I was afraid I loved it more than I would love the baby in it.

I pushed it gently and it rocked back and forth. I felt a shiver, and I pulled my duvet to my chin. There was something in the room. I felt it change. I closed my eyes and felt a wave of nausea. I saw him, his dark eyes up close. His hair fell to his shoulders and then curled toward me, pulling me in. He leaned forward and whispered, "Don't tell. Please don't tell." I woke up. I had fallen asleep and now I was awake and shaking. My back hurt. The clock said 12:19. I saw that the lights were out in the house. Everyone was asleep. Don't tell.

What did that mean? I felt something I hadn't felt in nearly ten months. I felt like I was starting my period. My lower back hurt. First, it was mild, but I couldn't sleep. I kept hearing him. Don't tell, please.

I wanted to go back to sleep and ask. But I had that low spreading discomfort. I dozed and then woke and noticed the clock. I sat up at 2:47. This was pain, this wasn't the kind you could sleep through. Maybe this was it. Was I in labor? I breathed through my nose until there was a subsiding of the pressure. My belly was hard as a bowling ball, and then soft again. I had had hundreds of those Braxton Hicks contractions in the last few weeks, but this ache was new. I watched the clock. Eight minutes later, it came again. I clenched my fists and then uncurled them. I lay there, waiting for the next contraction. Another seven minutes and it started. I wasn't afraid. I wanted to stay in my room as long as I could. I knew the rule. Five minutes apart, steadily, with pain. Would the next one be six, and then five and then right to four? Or would they waver and go back and forth, seven, then eight then nine and then six? I just had to wait and watch. Sure enough, the next one was eight minutes later, and I felt maybe I had a long night ahead of me.

I looked around my room and took it in, the last night it would be mine, alone. I thought about Grace. I thought about what she would think of me in this state. I wanted to call Gaby, but I was afraid this was just practice. I wasn't hurting that bad. I dozed for a few minutes and then counted the seconds when the next contraction came seven minutes later. It was now 3:29. I wasn't going to wake my parents up until it was necessary. I tried to conjure up my invisible boyfriend. Where was he now? When I had been pulled so furiously to that pond in the early morning, I had been able to feel his presence in the area. Now, where was he? I needed him. I needed God to be on my side. I could already feel the bubble surrounding me, in me, the love, the desire, my inner world, slipping out of reach. I cried out. Then I stopped myself. I didn't want my parents yet. I wanted to be alone just a little while longer. I had to get control over this. I lay in my bed and breathed in and out, I closed my eyes between the pains and let what came, come and go. I had learned to meditate in the recent months with Gaby. I had been able to wait and watch what came.

Now, in the dark, I had visions. It was Grace playing the viola, me cutting her hair, Grace in her long white nightgown. Then it was the funeral, me in black with bags under my eyes. Mrs. Adams, and then the boy in a black suit from behind. He was at the funeral. I thought he was Grace, from the back, with that hair. I reached to touch it. I felt the pain begin, and I sat up. I was nauseous now. It was 5:11. It had been six minutes since the last one. After the pain fell away again, I got up and went to my bathroom. I wanted to take a shower before we had to go. I turned the water on and got the towel ready. When I was totally wet, the pain came again. I placed my hands against the wall and let the water stream down. Somehow it seemed less intense in the water. I soaped up quickly, and soon there was another. They were coming

faster. I dried off and went to get my mother. It was still black
out. I knocked on the door and I heard her jump up,

"Eve? Come in."

My dad was stirring. My mom was sitting up.

"I think it's time."

"How? What?"

My mom got out of bed, and I braced myself against the
wall.

"They're every five minutes."

"Eve . . . five! Already! Why didn't you get me?"

"I wanted to wait to wake you."

"How long have you been up?"

"Since 12:30. I've been dozing off and on, all night . . .
and watching the clock."

My dad was up now.

"You took a shower?"

"Yeah."

"Eve, when was the last one?"

"5:47"

"That was four minutes ago."

"I think another one is coming."

"Oh my God."

"Mom, he said every five minutes for an hour. We are
fine."

"Sit down here on my bed. Paul, call the doctor. I'm going
to grab my things."

So, we all had our jobs. My mother jumped in the shower,
but she was ready in less than three minutes. She helped me

get a t-shirt dress on, and my dad got the bag. We drove as the sun was coming up. I hoped this would be over soon. I wasn't feeling so good. When we got to the hospital, I could barely stand. It seemed like they were coming one after another. The nurse got me a gown and we were given a room. My mother helped me put it on and I got in the bed, but I was agitated.

"I need something. This is horrible. I need the epidural," I wailed.

"We have to wait for the doctor to get here," the nurse, Shayna, said.

"I'm going to check you. We'll get something honey, he's on his way."

She took her hand and went inside me until I yelped.

"Okay, there now, relax. Look, you are already at five. Wow. You are doing great. As soon as he's here, we'll get the epidural."

I rocked. The contractions were every three minutes, hardly twenty seconds in between. I stopped talking. The doctor finally walked in the door.

"Eve, you ready for some relief?" I didn't answer.

"You're already five centimeters dilated. That's really progressing. I can give you an epidural. Do you want it?"

I nodded.

"Yes?"

"Yes!" my mother shrieked.

I signed the paper in an unknown scrawl, and I bent forward. I didn't care what they stuck in my back. My mother turned away. My father held my shoulders and whispered, "Be as still as you can. I've got you." I moaned.

"There. That's over. In a few minutes, you'll feel it kicking in. You'll see. You okay?"

"Yeah," I sputtered.

I lay back in the bed and breathed through my nose, and sure enough within ten minutes I felt the waves subside, the grip on my whole body loosened and became just a dull pressure. Then I sat up and smiled,

"Wow. That's the best thing that ever happened to me. Is it over?"

"Well, we have to let it taper off so you can push."

"This is amazing. I feel fine."

"I remember," my mother said. "I remember thinking no invention ever was better than the epidural."

"I think I can push just the way I am. See, I can move my legs."

"Well, you've got a ways to go."

"How long do you think?" I had an adrenaline rush. I could have run up and down the halls. I was ready to do my job.

"Hopefully a couple of hours. That would be a fast delivery."

And for about an hour I was pain-free and talkative. Then I started feeling the dull pain creeping around again.

"What's this? I'm starting to feel it again."

"I'm going to check you again. Then we can see about

getting you a booster."

"Okay, it's looking good. You're about eight already." And as soon as she said that a gush of liquid soaked me. The contraction was rolling over me and I felt like I would throw up.

"That's your water breaking. Now things should speed up really fast. Let me clean you up, honey."

"I need a booster."

"You're going to be ready to push real soon."

"I need the epidural back."

"Shayna? Can she get something?"

"I'll call him."

"There you are. Deep breaths."

She was right. After my water broke, it was like a train barreling forward. There was no break. I was clenched, trying to breathe deep breaths. I felt out of control.

The anesthesiologist arrived and I begged.

"Please. I can't take this."

"You're close. I'll give you a little to take the edge off. Then it will be time to push."

This time the relief was not so pure and ecstatic. I hardly felt any relief. I could barely handle the contractions, and I was worried that they would get worse. My mother held my hand until I pushed her away. I could not stand to be touched. Gaby had arrived with the speakers and the playlist. She had a tennis ball for my back, but I was not having any of that. She had been giddy when she arrived, but now she was trying to shrink into the chair. Maybe she was filming, but I did not look. I squeezed my eyes shut and moaned. I don't think this was what she expected. My mother was wincing as she felt my pain. She tried to console me by telling me that her mother had been in labor for 36 hours with her.

"So far, you've got record speed. It won't be that long." We had been in the hospital for only three and a half hours. Shayna checked me again and reported a ten. I was fully dilated.

"You can push now. Let's get this baby out."

I was so ready to hear this. I was going to gather my strength and push this baby out in one fell swoop. I was going to get it out if I had to go in there with my own hands. But it didn't happen like that. I took a breath and breathed and counted to ten, pushing so hard I felt the veins in my face standing out. I felt my cheeks hurt. I thought my skin would break.

"Good, good . . . focus, Eve. Push like you are going to the bathroom. Focus down."

No baby. Gaby was behind me now and my mom to my side.

"Relax and wait for the next contraction."

I wanted to throw up. They brought me a pan. But I did not . . . yet. There was another contraction and I inhaled and pushed again. This time I tried to concentrate on the area.

"Better. I can see the head."

"Eve, I can see the head," Gaby shouted. "It has dark hair."

Dark hair. Of course. I didn't have dark hair. No one in my family did. But I didn't care about hair or anything else. I vomited into a pan, and I moaned. I tried to push harder. I thought I couldn't possibly push any harder. But apparently, it wasn't good enough. I gave up. After an hour of pushing, and all those people in the room screeching, "It's right there. Just push hard. It's almost over." I kept saying I couldn't do it. I threw up again. It was the worst thing I ever hope to live through. I am never having another baby. Shayna had my mother get on one side and hold my legs back while Gaby was on the other. She had the camera in her hand, but she was not using it now. Shayna got in my face and said,

"Eve, the baby is right here. This time you are going to take a deep breath and push down hard and count to ten. You are going to keep pushing and finish. I know you can do it. Okay."

"I just can't," I wailed.

"Yes, you can. Eve, look at me. Here we go."

But I couldn't. The baby's heart rate plummeted, and I was too weak to push. They wheeled me into the operating room and covered my lower half with a blue sheet while my mom held my hand. Everything was fast. The pain was gone. Then there was some chatter from the other end of the bed and some pressure and, "It's a girl."

There was a thin cry. It was finally over. I closed my eyes and tried to shut out the noise. They whisked her away unlike in the movies I had seen where the baby was on the mother's chest. For a long time they were in a corner of the room. I didn't see. An alien, I thought. A monster. Served me right. It was too quiet. I just wanted to disappear. They could do something with it. Then my mother came over with a white burrito-looking bundle.

"Evie, look what you made. She's so beautiful."

I opened my eyes and saw her tiny face, watery eyes wide open, blinking . . . .at me. She was looking hard at me. Her mouth formed an O. She was serious looking and intense. I think she was mad at me for making her come out that way. She looked normal, human. My mother was in love. I was exhausted. They put her next to my face and I touched her cheek. Then I don't remember much. I closed my eyes and slept.

I woke up much later. It was dark out and my father was in the chair in the corner of the room. The lights were low, and my mother was not in the room. My dad looked up from the *Newsweek* he was reading. He took off his glasses.

"You're up."

"Where is everyone?"

"Mom went home to take a shower. She should be back anytime. Gaby went home a while ago. How do you feel?"

"Tired. Sore, I think. I can't move."

"I think that's normal. That's a lot of work you did."

"What about the baby?"

"She's in the nursery. They wanted you to rest. They'll bring her in soon."

"Is she okay?"

"Oh yeah. She's a beauty."

"Does she have any . . . problems?"

"She's perfect. She had the cord wrapped around her neck, but she is fine now. You're the one who scared us a little. But you will be good to go tomorrow."

"That was so much worse than I thought."

"Well, you did a great job, and now it's all over."

"Are you sure she's normal?"

"I promise. They'll bring her right back. You'll see."

I guess they knew what they were talking about. She was out of me. And I felt nothing. I still had a big stomach and there was no star in the sky, no media. It was quiet, and I didn't even know where she was. Was she going to leave me too? I felt my face get wet and my dad jumped up.

"Evie, are you in pain?"

I shook my head. "It's all okay, sweetie," he said. "You were so strong. Here, I'm going to call the nurse and have them bring you your girl."

Just then my mother came. She went out to the nurse's station and told them to bring the baby in. A different nurse—Shayna was gone—wheeled a plastic bassinet over to my bed. There was the burrito, tightly bound. A pink knit cap was on her head. She slept. It looked like a different baby than I remembered. The one I had seen in the delivery room had been old and wise. This one was soft and sweet.

"Do you want to hold her?" my mother asked.

I didn't want to wake her up. I shook my head.

"You won't wake her, She's out."

She picked her up and I watched her head loll a bit, her mouth move, a sniffle maybe, and then she was in the crook of my mother's elbow, still asleep. My mother sat down next to me.

"Why couldn't I get her out?"

"You were just exhausted and then her cord got compressed, so they wanted to get her out fast. You did an amazing job. Most people are in labor much longer."

"Who does she look like?"

"Mmm. I think a little like you did. Mostly herself. Look at her hair."

She pulled the cap off and I saw the abundance of nearly black, shiny, wispy hair.

"She doesn't look like us," I said.

"Oh, it's just the dark hair. It'll probably all fall out. Raine had dark hair when she was born. You can't tell at this age what it will look like later. She may have blond curls like you."

"I hope not." I turned away. "I'm really sleepy again."

My mother took the rocker and my dad said good night to us. I saw the look between them before I fell asleep again. It said, "Just what we thought. Now we have two babies."

When I woke up, it was morning again and my mother was still there dozing. She came to about the time the nurse came in with a bottle.

"Do you want to try to feed her?"

I turned my head. "No. I'm not ready." I was afraid of hurting her. I didn't know anything about babies. She was so small.

"Well, I'll leave a bottle here if she wakes up. You just call me, and I'll show you how to breastfeed when you are ready. It's really good for her if you can try."

My mother came to my side and helped me walk to the bathroom. It was like walking with a knife in my gut. She had to nearly carry me. By the time I saw myself in the mirror, I had sweat across my upper lip. I looked horrible. I washed my face and brushed my teeth, put a bit of moisturizer on and a thin film of foundation and lip tint with mom's help. I gathered my hair into a messy bun. I looked 100 percent better. I got back in bed. The baby slept next to me in her bin.

"Eve, I need to go home for an hour and get cleaned up. You're okay?"

My eyes widened. "What about her?"

"She'll be fine. If she cries, pick her up and try the bottle. Here's the button. If you need help getting up."

"Tell them to come get her. I can't be alone. I can't even get up alone."

I was just a kid. What were they thinking, leaving me with a newborn?

"If she wakes up, call the nurse. I will be right back. Eve, you're fine."

And, all of a sudden, it was my old mom, the no-

nonsense one. Get back on the horse, she was saying. She wanted me to have to pick up that baby and look at her. I sulked as she went out the door. She probably had a word with the nurse. After less than twenty minutes, the baby started to stir. I stiffened and watched her come to. Then there it was, the cry. At first, it was squeaky and weak, then it got stronger, and her face turned red. I pushed the button, and the nurse was there instantly.

"Need some help lifting? I know you're sore. I'll just help you bring her to the bed."

"No, you can take . . ."

"Here she is. Oh, she's a hungry girl. She's late for her breakfast. Here let me help you undo your gown."

"No . . . the bottle," I yelped.

And next thing I knew, she was there in my arm and the bottle was in my other hand, and then I lowered it to her open mouth and she got quiet. She sucked and blinked her eyes. "Give her two ounces, see right here, and then burp her on your shoulder. Pat her back until you hear a burp. You got it, you know what to do," and she was gone.

I looked down and the room fell away. The light from the window, the rocker, the door, everything disappeared at that moment as I looked down at her. I saw my tears splash down on her cheek and she turned her face up and looked at me. She stopped sucking and seemed to watch me. Then I saw the eyes. I saw *into* her eyes, and I saw what I was looking for.

I kept crying. I was in so much pain from the day before and my jerky sobbing was hurting me so much that I almost couldn't see, but I knew right then where she came from. I remembered the truth. How had I forgotten, covered up something so human with God? Where had I been for nine months? I was not a virgin. But I was not lying either. I didn't remember anything about him. Now I remembered everything. I knew the smell of that bed and the breeze from the window. I could feel the quilt. I could see the little dent in his forehead right here in this baby girl. The eyelids and the lashes. And, of course, that inky hair. She was baby Grace for a reason. Her father was the one at the funeral, in the kitchen, in the bed. Patrick was her father. Grace was her aunt. Grace *had* come through me, back to me in her own river, my river. We had been inseparable girls, and now she was back here in my baby girl, to go on with me forever. Grace had always been the leader between us, and now I would have to be the one to show this baby everything. As I put her to my shoulder and patted her back, I remembered the nights in Grace's room, the chill in the air, the pillow. I remembered the whisper of the bathroom door sliding open when he saw that I was in her bed. His whisper,

"Eve? Is that you?"

CHAPTER 16

Sparrow

I was afraid that as soon as Mrs. Adams saw her, she would know the truth. What if she had known all along . . . that Grace was coming back because her genes were now actually inside of me. I had abandoned Mrs. Adams in the last few months, thought she was crazy, but now I knew I was the crazy one. I gave the baby some more of the bottle and then her mouth became still, and a dribble of milk ran down the side. She made a scrunched face, and then went calm and peaceful. She was so beautiful, so perfect. She was a miracle. I always thought newborns were ugly and wrinkled and smelly. My baby was smooth and had plump cheeks and a rosebud mouth. She was special. I wondered if they were talking about it in the nursery, how unusual she was. The nurse came in then.

"Just checking on you."

"Um, she drank it . . . the two ounces. And she burped."

"Good. Now she's happy. You're a pro."

"Is it okay if I unwrap her?"

"She's your baby. Look at her. Count her toes. Go ahead. Get to know her. She's beautiful."

"I know. I mean she really is, isn't she?"

"She's a keeper."

"She is *unusually* pretty, isn't she?"

"Mm-hmm. Don't tell the others, though. I can't have favorites."

I unwrapped the blanket and looked at her little body. Her legs were bent, as they must have been inside me. Her little toes were all there. Her feet looked like my doll, Jessie, the only one I ever had. She was warm and pink, and she made little squeaks every now and then. Her arms jerked like she was trying to catch herself in a fall. I tried to wrap her back up in the burrito, but I couldn't do it. Her foot stuck out one side and her hands were free. Then my mother walked in. I gasped. I was scared to tell her what I knew. She walked over to me smiling.

"Look at you, doing great."

"I fed her."

"Well, she looks happy."

"Isn't she really pretty?"

"Beautiful. She looks like you now."

"No. She doesn't look like me at all."

"She does. I'll show you a picture of you. You have the same mouth."

"I think she looks like Grace."

"You mean the black hair?"

"Everything. She looks like her."

I saw the look cross her face. Dr. Phillips would be called.

Was she putting me on? Did she really not see it? Was she in denial too?

"How do you feel?"

"Better."

"You look better."

"Is it normal for her to sleep so much?"

"Oh yeah, give her a few weeks. She's still exhausted."

"Did you call Mrs. Adams?"

"Yes. I told her you were still uncomfortable. She would like to come visit."

"Was she so happy it was a girl?"

"Yeah. She said she was sure it was a girl. You know she is dying to see her."

"I can't get her wrapped up again."

"Here," my mother said, knowing just what to do.

"I was never good at this, but this is how you do it. Take this corner and pull it over here, then put her arms down, like this, then the other corner goes across and up here, like this. And it's supposed to be tighter, but that's the idea."

"You know all this."

"Well, I've done it twice."

"And you remember?"

"I guess so."

"Do you think I should breastfeed?"

"Well, you have to do what you feel comfortable doing. But I think you should try it."

"I feel stupid. It's embarrassing."

"Even if you are alone?"

"It seems so . . . unnatural."

"It just seems odd because you haven't even had breasts for very long. You might find it just fine. The bottles are a nuisance. They have to be sterilized and heated and all that. In the middle of the night, it's pretty great just to pick her up and go. And it's good for her immune system."

"I guess I'll try."

"I'm glad you are holding her. It's the best thing in the world, holding a new baby. She is 100 percent perfect, you know? Later she will have been touched by the world for good and for bad. But right now, she is pure perfection . . . just pure."

"Yeah. I never got it."

"What?"

"I never understood what was great about a newborn. I thought they were ugly and strange, and people just waited for them to get cute."

"Well, she's yours. It makes all the difference."

"She's special, though. The nurse agreed."

"Of course she is."

I wanted to be alone with Mrs. Adams when she saw the baby for the first time. I wanted to see her reaction without my mother there. For now, I had chosen her name: Sparrow. I wasn't absolutely sure yet, but I wanted a name for her that came from nature, like my name. I didn't like Summer or River or Sky. They were too common, too obvious. Her name was so important. On Easter, I had been in the garden listening to the birds and I thought of how wonderful to be able to make those songs and to fly. My baby bird. I wanted her to fly. I was weighing it heavily. Today she was Sparrow Grace. Mrs. Adams would probably think Sparrow was weird and stupid. She said she liked Serafina and Rebecca. I wouldn't tell her until after she had seen her and told me whether she looked like Grace as I thought.

I asked my mother to go get me something sweet from The Cupcake, my favorite bakery. It was on the other side of town. I was going to eat something other than Jell-O and broth for the first time in days. And she was happy to go out and get something special for me even if it was far. She would be gone for a little while. Mrs. Adams knocked on the door softly, and pushed it open with her free hand. In the other, she held a perfect coconut cake, high and topped with pink booties that I knew she had sculpted out of marzipan. I should have known she'd bring a cake. Cake—coconut, my favorite—and the most excited person to see my new baby, all at once. She hugged me before she peered into the bassinet. Sparrow was sleeping, but I told her she could pick her up. She tenderly slid her hand under the baby's neck and opened her mouth in an O when the baby yawned.

"Oh goodness, she is just . . ." and tears welled up in her eyes. Then she lifted her out and sat on the bed next to me. I pulled off the little striped cap, and her crown of dark hair was exposed.

"She's so beautiful," she said. "So, so perfect."

I waited for more, and she just looked, running her

fingers over her cheek and her hair and her little shell ear.

"Tell me about the birth. How bad was it?"

"I thought I was dying. It was the worst."

"I remember. After I gave birth to Patrick, I went back to read the section of the Bible that dealt with Eve's breach of trust, and the pain that women would suffer bringing forth children. I had somehow imagined that when the baby was coming, there would be a euphoric moment when I would look down and feel him come in a great, wonderful burst of strength, not agony and nausea and sweat. They kept telling me to look down, and I felt like throwing up, and I didn't care what there was to see. I had pictured myself reaching down and pulling him to my chest, when really, I just fell back and listened to them say, "It's a boy!!!" I was sure I was dying. The joy came when it was all over. I sat up to see him, and I realized I was finally pain-free. Was it like that for you? I hadn't listened carefully to the scriptures about pain. It had been wrenching pain until he was fully free of me. There is sadness in that, I know. It seems that it should be hard work to deliver your baby into the world, but not sheer agony. "

"It was agony all right."

"It should feel glorious, like reaching the peak of Everest. But the pain reminds us of God and we survive it. We are more powerful than we know. And it's so worth it. Look what you got."

"Yeah. I can say that, now that it's all over."

"Yes, then you do feel like a warrior. Patrick was so beautiful to me that I cried on his face, and I swear he was drowning in my tears. He was big and plump and had beautiful, long eyelashes. I will never forget his first day on earth. When I fed him, I knew why I had been born. I thought I would have ten babies after that. But after Grace was born, I had to have a tumor removed from my uterus, and I was unable to have another child. I know I was blessed to have a boy and a girl, both so healthy and pretty. I was grateful, but I did feel cheated about never being able to be pregnant again or have another baby in my arms. Those were the best years of my life."

"I hope I will feel that way."

"I've never seen such a beautiful baby," she said again, touching Sparrow's cheek.

"What about Grace?" I whispered.

"Oh, Grace was the sweetest thing, but she was bald and a little blotchy at first. She wasn't beautiful for a couple of months. Now Patrick . . . he looked almost as pretty as this angel."

My heart started beating fast.

"I really thought she looked like Grace," I said.

"She feels like Grace, all light and delicate. Have you decided what to name her?"

"Sparrow."

"Oh, that's different."

"She is my little bird. If you don't mind, I would like her middle name to be Grace."

"Oh Eve, I would love that. Sparrow Grace. It's both unique and classic."

"I wanted to see her before I named her, and when I saw her, it seemed right."

"You are very creative, and thoughtful as always."

"I still think she looks like Grace."

Mrs. Adams looked at me carefully. Without taking her eyes off me, she said, "If I ever have a granddaughter, I hope she is as precious as Sparrow Grace." I couldn't take it anymore. Her face was right next to mine and when she said the word granddaughter, I began to shiver. I fell against the pillow and tried to breathe. What did she know? Could she know about Patrick? Was it obvious?

"You're very pale, Evie. Do you need something?"

"I don't feel so good. Can you press the call button? I can't get a breath."

"Let me call the nurse."

And as she did, I fell back, and closed my eyes. By the time the nurse got there, I was sweating and she took my pulse and helped me calm down with a sedative. She turned to Mrs. Adams and said, "I think we should let her sleep. She has had enough excitement for now." And Mrs. Adams put Sparrow back in the bed and left, as the nurse watched my heart rate slow. I drifted off. I didn't want to wake up. This time I let myself see his face beyond the eyes and hair. I reached for his long hair and pulled, and I saw him in front of me, not Jesus, not God, not the angel Gabriel or Grace. Just Patrick Adams, his handsome, popular, off-center smile, his white teeth, his beautiful dark hair. Patrick before the accident, smooth and easy, happy-go-lucky Patrick. His hands against my stomach, on my hips. His mouth on mine. It all came back to me.

* * *

It was after I had been sneaking into the house for several weeks. He had come into the bathroom and stood at the door as I remained perfectly still, trying to disappear. He didn't seem frightened.

"Eve?" he whispered in the dark.

"Yeah?" I whispered back.

He came over to the bed.

"How long have you been here?"

"Not long."

"I heard the window. I think I've heard it before. Have you come here before?"

"Yeah."

"I kept hearing something in the middle of the night."

"I can't sleep. I always wake up around 2:00, so I came here one night, and I fell asleep for a few hours. Now it's kind of a habit."

"I wake up too. Actually, I don't really sleep much."

"Do you think about her?"

"Yeah."

"Is it bad?"

"I keep seeing the car . . . and the dark, and feeling that cold water. I can't get it out of my mind."

"I'm sorry. I'm sorry you had to be there. I just miss her."

"Me too. I didn't even appreciate her. I just ignored her."

"You're her brother. That's the way it is."

"But when we were little . . . we were best friends, and then I kind of left her behind."

"She loved you. She knew you loved her. Most brothers and sisters hate each other. You guys were luckier."

"Were . . . we *were* lucky. Not anymore. Why do you think it had to happen to her? She was so good. I . . . I am not nearly as good as Grace, and I didn't die. Do you know what I mean? Why her?"

"You know what your mother thinks."

"That she was chosen. God wants only the best."

"Mmm."

"Do you believe that?"

"What else is there? God is mean, cruel, evil?"

"Or just a terrible accident. Or God sucks," he said.

That night we talked. The next night, I asked him if he would lay down next to me. For several nights we slept side by side, waking before the sun came up. I would slide the window up, and he would wake up. I finally felt calm. Then one night he put his arm around me. Then the next night, he held me again. I barely remember how it happened. We became so close, just warm and close, and then I don't know . . . we were tangled. I don't even remember how it felt. I don't remember pain or joy or anything at all. It was like a dream. It just felt safe and warm. Then it happened once more, I think. Then I went to North Carolina on a bus, and I forgot everything. Full-on amnesia. I would have told Gaby if I had remembered. But I did not. Instead, I found a deep pond and fell in, and found God to make my pregnancy make sense to me, if to no one else. I came home and I didn't need to sleep in Grace's bed anymore. I didn't remember anything about being with Patrick, only the face in my dreams coming in and out, the dramatic hair, the eyes.

Was I an idiot? How could I not see him? I knew it was Grace's hair, eyes. I knew it was a boy, a man. So how did I decide that boy was Jesus instead of Patrick Adams, I want to know. No one could have that much denial. My brain must have been working like crazy to shut it all out. Completely. Even seeing him in the Adamses' kitchen occasionally had not triggered memories of our time together in her bed. I did not ever think of Patrick as my baby's father. I had completely put him away; the nights in the dark with him had disappeared. I had created my own story. And I believed it wholly. Even when I had run into Patrick, I had had an odd feeling, but I thought it was only awkward because I reminded him of her. I kept going over to their house, never once ashamed to face Mrs. Adams. I had squashed those nights with Patrick, conveniently replacing him with God. I had taken care of my end of the story.

What was HE thinking? I assumed Mrs. Adams kept my secret and did not tell Patrick that I was pregnant. I had not seen him in months, since before I was really showing. Did he know I had mono? Did he even know I was missing from school? Did he know all along that I was wearing a puffy vest to cover my body, and was he avoiding me? Had he sent Taylor to talk to me? Was he shaking in his boots, knowing I was there in the kitchen with his mother every week? God help me. God help him. I didn't ever want to wake up from that dream, the story I spun. It was a fairy tale for my spiraling situation.

But the end has arrived. I am not a virgin bride. Sparrow *is* Beth Adams's granddaughter. Mrs. Adams had been so sure that Grace was coming back to us through this baby, and she was not wrong. I had been so sure that God had chosen me to bear this child, come to earth to make things right. Now the baby is here, a girl that looks like Patrick, not God. And Mrs. Adams even said the words "my granddaughter" to me. If she knew, she didn't seem upset. She seemed to glow. Had she known before I had? Maybe all along she knew about us. Maybe she had seen us. Maybe she was trying to tell me. Or maybe she just wanted a baby girl to love, however it came.

When I did wake up and force my eyes open, it was getting dark out, and my mother was in the rocker, holding Sparrow. Mrs. Adams was gone.

"You're awake. You slept a long time."

"Yeah, I felt very out of breath, all of a sudden."

"Beth said you were having a panic attack, and the nurse had to give you a sedative. Did something happen when she was here?"

"I just got really dizzy and my heart was pounding."

"Do you feel better?"

"I think so. I'm hungry."

"Yeah, I guess so. I brought your brownie and I see you have a whole cake."

"She made it for us."

"For you."

"What did Mrs. Adams say?"

"She was worried about you. She was worried she wore you out. She thinks the baby is gorgeous, you know, she was gushing over her a lot."

"She doesn't think she looks like Grace."

"Was she disappointed?"

"No. She seemed really happy."

"Did you think Mrs. Adams would think she might replace Grace . . . in some way?"

"I don't know."

"Do *you* think she might sort of be some replacement for Grace? Maybe that is why you wanted her so badly?"

"Mom. I don't think she is Grace."

"Okay." My mom exhaled. She was happy to hear that I guess.

"How do you feel now, now that she is here?"

"Just tired, but good. I love her already."

"I knew you would. Do you feel a little more relaxed?"

"Maybe. I think there are some things I had forgotten."

"Do you want to tell me about it?"

"I don't know for sure what I feel right now."

"Well, you can always tell me whatever you feel. It doesn't

have to be for sure."

"I thought she was going to have some aura about her. I thought everyone would see her and say, 'Oh . . . I get it.' I thought it would be obvious that there was something miraculous about her, you know. Or I thought maybe she wouldn't even be human."

"Ahh. You were scared."

"Scared, but also hopeful that there would be an explanation for her."

"And now?"

"I think I know. And it's nothing miraculous."

"You know?"

I closed my eyes. My mother waited.

"I don't want to talk about it right now."

"Eve, it's okay. Everything is okay. You tell me when you are ready."

"Will you call Dr. Phillips tomorrow?"

"Of course. Would you like to see her?"

"I think so. Do you think Sparrow is the right name?"

"I think it's precious. Sweet little bird."

I held her in my arms and tried to breastfeed her when the nurse came to help, and my mother was gone for the night. It was weird; like all of a sudden, your thumb is making orange juice when before it was just a finger. Weird. But when she settled in, it was relaxing, and it didn't feel so strange. The bad part was getting her to latch on. I didn't like that part. But she was pretty good at it, so I figured I'd get over it. And it was convenient. Food anywhere, anytime. I ate my cake. I watched her sleep. So far, she had been a quiet baby. I only heard her cry once when she was hungry. Of course, I had been asleep and my mom was there tending to her needs. I was feeling better now and was down to Tylenol for the pain. I was going home the next day.

Tonight, I was alone in the room with her for the first time. My mother was doing her sink or swim thing. I knew I had to tell her the truth about Patrick. I wanted to see Dr. Phillips first. I wanted to know why I had been unable to remember such a huge thing, and why I could remember now. Maybe I was mentally ill. What if I just forget that I have a baby one day and leave her in the car or in the park? Surely there is something wrong with me, having amnesia for ten months, and what if they try to take her away from me if I am crazy. My parents are going to be disappointed. I think they would be happier not knowing that Patrick Adams is involved. I think they were beginning to believe that I really had done this alone. I know they will blame Mrs. Adams somehow.

She started to stir. Her little cry was getting stronger. I knew she would let out a full scream if I didn't get to her quick. It hurt to get out of bed and then pick her up, but I did it, as she thrashed her little arms. The blanket came undone as I arranged myself in the dark room lit only by the moon. "Hold on, I'm going as fast as I can," I whispered. I got the gown unsnapped and pulled her to me, looking down as little as possible. She was like a suction cup when she got to me. Then it got quiet, and she was still, and I watched her little cheek pump, pump, and then rest. She was so cute like this, with her eyes closed, knowing just how to feed herself. That was cool. I had done it. She cried. I fed her. She would survive. Maybe I would, too. I was really doing it. I could take care of a baby. Eve London manufactures milk. This was too much.

I could see why this breastfeeding thing was so popular. In the middle of the night, when I heard the rustling, and I just wanted to sleep, I pictured myself having to crawl out of bed, listen to the cries escalate, crawl downstairs and wait for a bottle to heat. This way, I just pulled her to me and lay back and closed my eyes. It was almost like sleeping. It was the way to go. It's still weird, though, and my boobs are so huge, I think there may be something really wrong. I mean, when I finally took a shower, I had to stare. I look like one of those porn stars. They do not look real. I never wanted boobs. They are hard to run with, so I really hope they go away. Mom says, *Don't worry about that!*

Dr. Phillips came to see me. She held Sparrow while we talked. I never pictured her for the baby type. Then she told me she has a four-year-old. I never knew. She'd like to have another, but it hasn't happened, she said. I saw then how unselfish she had been listening to me, watching me grow a baby that wasn't planned when she wanted one. It made me think about all the people out there wanting babies, and all the people like me, who should give them up, but can't. It's too late now. If I hadn't seen her, maybe I could have done it, but not now.

"I think I know what happened to me," I said.

"Okay." Dr. Phillips looked up at me from the baby. She waited.

"I'm afraid to say."

"It's frightening?"

"No, but it will hurt people, and I am embarrassed."

"You've been hurt already."

"I'm embarrassed because I remember what happened, and I'm not actually a virgin. I know now exactly when it happened. But I swear, I only remembered everything when I went into labor and felt pain, and then when I saw her. I wasn't lying."

I told her the whole story. All about the window and the bed, and Patrick and I whispering in the night. How he held me, and I finally felt relief.

"I still don't know how that waterfall and God and the dreams fit in. But I believed it all. I really did. I had a baby because I thought I was special. If I had known it was Patrick, I would have had an abortion, I'm sure of it. Does this mean I am crazy?"

"The mind works hard to protect you. No, it means you were so raw and in grief that your mind protected you from more trauma."

"But what if it was my way of bringing Grace back to us? She's her niece, her blood. Isn't that crazy? I want to believe I was still chosen, kind of, to keep her alive."

"That makes sense. And in other ways, you *were* chosen,

Eve. I want a baby, and I haven't been able to have one. You were. It makes a 39-year-old doctor think, that's for sure. Does Mrs. Adams know?"

"No, but she came to see us, and she said Sparrow was as pretty as Patrick was when he was born, which made me wonder."

"Does Patrick know?"

"I haven't seen him in months. I'm sure Mrs. Adams didn't tell him I was pregnant. She wouldn't have broken my trust like that. We never talked about it, but she said she hadn't told anyone but her husband."

"But he knows that he had sex with you."

"Well, if he is not crazy like I was."

"Do you think he's been avoiding you?"

"I would be."

"He's never tried to talk to you in school?"

"No. But I never see him there. It's a huge school. We don't have any classes together. I saw him at the house maybe two or three times over the year. I thought he looked at me kind of strangely. And he said something once, that I looked different. But his mother was there, and I was just thinking he was Grace's popular brother as always, and I was shy around him. I ignored him, so I guess he thought I wanted him to leave me alone. I just don't know."

"Are you going to tell him?"

"I have to. He's going to die."

"He won't die any more than you did. He will have to get used to it. Have you thought about why you were able to be so intimate with him?"

"He knew what I was feeling. He was the only one who did, and that made him close to me then. So, I felt something very strong and . . ."

"Yes?"

"And he made me feel like I had someone to hold onto. He filled that emptiness where Grace had been."

It was so obvious, so ridiculously simple. That little moment that had filled each of us, the ability to forget, a few minutes without the hole in our hearts, or Grace herself, his black silky hair for me, my rosin-scented hands for him. It had led us here, to this room in a hospital with a psychiatrist and a baby girl; my life turned inside out.

"I think you see now."

"I see."

Maybe he didn't take her place, but he filled it. He covered the emptiness in me, if only for a moment or two. I must have done the same for him. He was handsome and popular and adored by girls. He saw something else in me, of course, probably just comfort, but I was her best friend, and that had to devastate him. I felt a wave of grief and suffering take me. I imagined the extra guilt Patrick must have felt when I disappeared and never came back. No wonder he ran laps and never came home. How did he go on? First, the accident, then me ignoring him, shaming him. I had conjured up a beautiful story that let me go on. What about Patrick?

I wanted to see him without anyone knowing. I told Dr.

Phillips to ask the nurse to take the baby. I needed to be alone. I needed to find him so we could talk before our mothers got involved.

"Eve. You are starting a new life. You have a very supportive family and it will work out. It won't be easy, but you will be fine. You have solved your own question. Now you can move on."

"He won't get in trouble, will he?"

"You mean, legally?"

"Yeah."

"You were both minors. And you say it was mutual."

"Yes."

"He won't get in trouble."

"Except for his parents."

"Eve, why do you think he risked that in Grace's bed, down the hall from his parents?"

"You think he wanted to get caught?"

"Do you?"

"No, but maybe he wanted to be blamed."

(PATRICK)

I tried to kill myself more than once. When they took away the pills they gave me after the accident, I couldn't sleep. I was so wired and just dead inside, it would have been easier to die. I didn't care what the Bible says about taking your own life. Hell could not be worse than what I was living. I found stronger pills from people at school, an assortment that knocked me out so I could escape my mind. When I took a whole handful, though, I just threw them up. I couldn't cut myself. I had the razors in my hand, but I couldn't do it. I am a wimp. So, I just kept moving. I ran and jumped and lifted and ate to keep going. I bought Xanax and weed to calm me at night and became the son my parents feared most. I stayed out late and got help with school from girls when they said I'd have to quit lacrosse. People helped me. I cheated. There was always a girl willing to help me keep up. Addie, of course, and when she was gone, Sophie, Megan, Laurel. I tried not to mislead them. I told them all that I had a girlfriend at church. That's how I got by. My friends Jake and Taylor kept an eye on me. When Gracie died, I hated waking up every day knowing I was alive, and she wasn't. I couldn't save her, and I was the only one there to do it. I couldn't reach her. I kept diving, but I couldn't hold my breath and I couldn't see. It was so dark. Afterward, I begged God to take me too. I wish I had just stayed down there with her. But my body told me to surface. It screamed to live.

No one blamed me, or my mother, who was driving. But I

know we are both to blame. Yeah, it was an accident, but we should have stayed home that night. My mother wanted us to see my cousin's play at church. We didn't want to go. We had homework. You didn't say no to my mother. It was raining hard. She said she had a migraine when we got in the car and I wanted to drive, but I only have my permit, and she wouldn't let me. I should have called my dad. I should have gotten to Grace first, and I should never have left the car in the water, or I should have thought to open the door instead of worrying about my mother. I was trying so hard to get us out, and I knew we were sinking, and I swam out, but then the car was just gone. And at the play, I went out back with some guys and had some vodka from a water bottle. So, I know I was slow. I was just too slow to save her. And all at once I became an only child.

I don't ever remember life without Grace. We were a year apart. I don't remember her coming home and invading my life like some people say happens. She was always there, quiet and serious and sweet. She was the best sister you could ask for. She loved me. And sometimes I ignored her. She was weird and embarrassing in high school, and I didn't stand up for her the way I should have. She needed a better protector. She was so serious and good and innocent. She really believed the stuff my mother preached. She loved Jesus with all her heart, a devotion I know nothing of. So, I have to wonder if that is why I am left here to live out this painful life. I may be being punished for my lack of devotion. And she is maybe forever in Heaven, a beautiful place. That is why I keep going to church and listening. That, and the fact that I am forced to, of course. But what kind of cruel God would go to those lengths to prove His existence to me? If that is God, then I hate Him. I can only live if I close my eyes and believe that Grace is forever swimming in the clear blue-green water that we saw in the Bahamas when I was in seventh grade and she was in sixth. I remember her clearly saying, sitting on the beach, braiding the hair of the little girls surrounding her, that this was Heaven. So, I tell myself she is there in the clear water and the warm sun, surrounded by her angels. If I didn't believe that, then I would have to go to bed and stay there, or run until I dropped.

I was at my worst in the fall of last year when I heard a noise in Grace's room one night. I had not been in her room since the accident, but I went to look since I was not sleeping, as usual. When I saw Eve in her bed, I thought she was Grace, haunting me, and I went cold for a moment. But when she spoke, I knew it was Eve, and I can't say I was surprised. It was odd, but I knew she was suffering almost as much as I was. My mother told me this. I realized then that she was the only other person in the world that I could talk to about Grace. And she had come to my house when we could talk alone. My parents were medicated, drugged on the other side of the house. They wouldn't wake up. So, we did. We talked about Gracie and about not sleeping and feeling all edgy and headachy all the time, and falling asleep in class. I liked Eve well enough. I had never noticed her really, before. I looked through her as she walked through my kitchen and the school halls. *She was nothing but my sister's tomboy friend. She was not unattractive; I just never looked at her face for all that tangled hair. Those nights, I looked. And I saw the bones in her jaw and her full lips and clear glass eyes. I saw that her eyelashes were black and long even though her hair was blondish. I wanted to hold her. But I tried to just talk. Then she asked me to lie down next to her. I slept next to her, and she smelled so clean. We were just holding on to each other. That's all I thought of. She was warm and safe. I didn't mean to hurt her.*

When she stopped coming to Grace's room all of a sudden, I was stunned. I thought we were helping each other, but now she was avoiding me. She disappeared. I was shamed beyond words. She wouldn't look at me in school. And I didn't dare hurt her more. I tried to forget, but I had nightmares about her. I thought I did even more damage. So, I kept moving. Soccer season was ending, and the Christmas season began. I hate that time of year now, a lull in sports, and I'm an only child at Christmas. It sucks. So, I trained more. I ran laps indoors and lifted weights. I came off the drugs gradually, hoping to get a scholarship. All of that working out made me sleep better. Addie and I hung out a little. I never saw Eve. Then one night she was in my kitchen. She looked different. I tried to get her attention with my eyes, but she made an excuse to leave. She truly was avoiding me. I thought about it. We had that brief time together because of our shared grief over Grace. It helped me. I hope it helped her too. But really, I guess that was all it was, and she had moved on, or she was ashamed and could not face me. I just feel bad about what happened. She seems so young and innocent. I felt her hold on to me so hard, I think I mistook it for wanting me, and I should have known better. Grace would be horrified. But I can't take it back now. And it was a long time ago.

Then I answered the phone one day, and it was her voice that I didn't even recognize. She had to say, "It's Eve."

"Oh," *I said, like an idiot.* "Hey Eve."

"I'm glad you answered the phone."

"Are you calling for my mom?"

"No. I am calling you."

"Hey, I wanted to talk to you awhile back, but I thought you might hate me."

"Why?"

"You seemed to be avoiding me."

"That's why I'm calling. I wasn't avoiding you. I kind of forgot . . . or actually I erased what happened with us. In Grace's room."

I didn't say anything.

"I just remembered everything," *she said.*

"Oh God. I'm sorry, Eve. It was all my fault."

"No. It wasn't. I just made it go away because I had suffered a trauma and my brain was playing tricks. And now I remember everything. I have to tell you something important though. I just had a baby."

"What?"

"I had a baby five days ago. She's your baby."

"*No.*"

"*I'm sorry to hit you with this all at once. I've had nine months to figure it out. I thought maybe you guessed I was pregnant. Your mother knew, but she said she wouldn't tell anyone. And she doesn't know about you, of course.*"

"*I need to sit down. I feel kind of . . . hold on a minute.*"

I put the phone down and put my head between my knees. I breathed until I could sit up, and then I took the phone to my room.

"*Sorry. I'm sorry. Are you saying it's mine?*"

"*Well, yes. You're the only one.*"

"*How can you have a baby?*"

"*She's right here. A girl.*"

"*And it's my baby?*"

"*Well, unless I forgot about someone else. But I know I didn't. I remember everything now. Sparrow looks like you. Even your mother said so.*"

"*My mother saw her?*"

"*She came to see me at the hospital. She doesn't know anything about you though. I promise.*"

"*Sparrow?*"

"*Her name is Sparrow. Sparrow Grace.*"

"*My heart is beating really hard.*"

"*It will be okay, Patrick. I've been through all of this months ago, and I promise it will be okay. I'm going back to school in the fall. My parents will help me. We don't have to tell anyone you are her father. No one would understand. And we're not going to live together or anything. We'll just go on, or you will, like always. I just needed to tell you that I remembered everything, and that you have a baby girl. And I'm sorry I didn't know a long time ago."*

"God, Eve."

"Don't worry."

"Don't worry! Do your parents know?"

"Not about you. But I told my therapist. She said she'd let me tell them. I am going to ask them not to tell your mother. I think they will listen . . . but I can't be sure."

"My parents will freak."

"Maybe they won't have to know," Eve said.

"Of course they will know. Why do you want to protect me, Eve?"

"I don't know. I feel like I made the decision to keep the baby. It's my decision and I am living with it, but you didn't."

"I made the decision to sleep with you. I shouldn't have."

"Me too. But I don't regret it."

"You were only fifteen."

"You were only sixteen."

"Your parents are going to kill me."

"They've already been through the worst. This will be the most normal part of what I've put them through. I need to talk to them now. It may take me a few days."

"Will you call me after?"

"Yeah. Then you can see her."

I hung up and beat my head against the mattress.

So that is that. I am a father. Seventeen years old. I don't even have my actual driver's license yet, and I have a baby girl named Sparrow. Is there a reason for everything? Am I being punished over and over for what I did to Grace? Or is this just a teenage pregnancy born out of my impulsive, selfish lust, and doing everything I could to reject my mother and her bullshit? I finally got what I deserve. I deserve much worse though. I didn't save her, and I fucked her best friend.

CHAPTER 17

Biology

I smashed his already broken heart. He sounded like he wanted to die. But when he sees her, he will see what I see, that she is the good thing in all this. She is the answer. I just know it. My Sparrow is an angel. She eats and she sleeps. She doesn't even cry hardly at all. Even my mother is suspicious. She never had a baby that didn't cry. So, I know that she is a special baby, not like Raine or me. When Patrick holds her and watches her breathe in and out and touches her tiny fingers, he will feel better.

After we talked, I let another day go by and my parents and I went to Dr. Phillips' office so I could tell them the truth. I needed her support and her explanation to get me through it.

"Oh my God. I don't know what to say," my mother gasped.

"He didn't do this to me. It was mutual. We were both in a lot of pain."

"Eve had what is called selective amnesia," Dr. Phillips said. "She experienced an initial trauma from losing a beloved friend. And then she tried to cope by going to Grace's room and immersing herself in her surroundings and her faith. When she and Patrick comforted each other there, it led to sex. And then when she suspected she was pregnant, it was too much for her brain and nervous system. Her mind was able to take an experience in nature in North Carolina and give her a false visual about what happened to her. It temporarily solved her dilemma. She was ashamed and needed a safer story, a magic story, kind of. She only remembered the reality when she went into labor. The pain brought back her memory."

My father looked pale. My mother had that look of panic cross her face, the kind that puts her on her feet to go and take care of the problem. I spoke up.

"I went to his house in the middle of the night to be in Grace's room over and over, and then he came in to talk to me and I slept next to him when I was feeling so bad, I couldn't sleep. We comforted each other. I am sorry that I couldn't tell you this a long time ago, but I blocked it all out until I was in labor. That's when I remembered. Please don't tell his parents. Please let him get used to this and leave Mrs. Adams out of it for now."

"I don't know what to say," my mother stuttered. "I am beyond shocked. And Eve, you don't need to protect him. You carried this baby for nine months and left school. He can join in now. He needs to pay the price the same way you have."

"I am not paying a price. I have a beautiful, perfect baby. I don't regret a thing."

"You are barely sixteen years old. This is the easy part.

Everything is ahead of you. You see how it goes when you are in school and trying to do homework and your one-year-old is destroying your room. You see how you feel when she has a fever of 102 and you are up all night and you have SATs the next morning. This is just the beginning. I love this baby already like she is mine, but Patrick Adams is going to share this responsibility, like it or not."

"He knows that. Please just wait a little. Just give us a little time. I am not ready for Mrs. Adams to be involved."

"Oh, she'll be involved all right, just like she wanted all along. And just you watch her change her tune when her own God-fearing child is a teenage father. You see how she takes it now, when the Virgin Mary theory is all shot to hell."

"Meredith!" my father gasped.

"I'm sorry, Eve. You can take some time, but I need to take some too. I never expected this."

"I want him to come over today and see her. You will be civil, right?"

"He should most definitely see her. I need to go for a drive."

"Thank you for telling us everything. Everything will be okay," my dad said, as is his way. It wasn't as bad as I thought. Sparrow slept through the whole ordeal in her car seat. When we got home, I called Patrick and told him my parents were gone and he could come over if he wanted. When I opened the door and saw him, my jaw literally dropped. He had cut his hair into a short crewcut. He wasn't the Patrick in my dreams, the beautiful Jesus figure, at all. I wouldn't have recognized him from across the street.

"Hi," he said shyly.

"Hi. I almost didn't recognize you with your hair."

"Oh. It's growing out. I shaved my head for the team."

"You look really different."

"Yeah? I wanted a fresh start, but it didn't help. You look the same. You don't look like you had a baby."

"Well, don't look too close," I said, covering my stomach with my hands.

"Come in here. She's in my room."

"I don't know if I can do it yet . . . see her."

"Um, okay . . . do you want something to drink?"

"Okay."

We went into the kitchen, and I got us La Croix waters. We sat at the island.

"I want to see her, I do, but I need a moment. My heart hasn't stopped pounding. I feel like it might explode. I think I have to calm down before I see a baby."

"You don't have to tell anyone she is yours. I'm serious."

"I have to. I have to tell my parents," Patrick said.

"I can tell them with you. I can explain what happened, and about my amnesia, and that it wasn't your fault."

"No. I have to tell them myself."

"What about school? Your friends?"

"It'll be weird."

"Because of me."

"No, not you. Because there is a baby, and we are teenagers and . . . Grace."

"If it were Addie Hill's baby, it wouldn't be so weird I guess."

"Well, I think it would be, but you were my sister's best friend. Don't you see how it looks? Like I took advantage of you. I didn't even know you before you came to Grace's room."

"No. But I asked you to lie down with me."

"Why do I feel like I hurt you?"

"You didn't. We made a mistake together. But now I don't even think it was a mistake. It's just a detour."

"I am going to talk to my minister's son. He'll tell me what to do."

"Okay."

"I will come back and see her. Soon, I promise. I just need a little time. I don't want to put any of my bad . . . my ugliness, near her now. I feel toxic. I want to clean some things up first."

I walked him to the door. "I'm really sorry," he said. "For everything."

I thought he would feel better. But I was wrong. I didn't want to cry. I really tried to keep it together. Then I shut the door and heard her rustling and felt my breasts leaking and my fat tears plopping on my shirt, and the spell was broken. I got her out of her bed and went out to the porch and let the sun shine on my face as I fed her. I was a wreck, but she was happy. I guessed that was the way it would be. Then my mother came home and sat beside me, and she had wet spots on her shirt too from her tears, and red eyes, and there we were, the three of us in our little train wreck. This is what I had done to my mother, and my daughter would probably do these hard things to me. I just started too early, that's all.

Patrick called me three days later, in the morning. He had just told his parents that Sparrow was his baby. His mother had to breathe into a bag, which gave his silent father something to do. The minister's son, Timothy, had been there to ease the shock. When she recovered, Mrs. Adams said just what she was thinking:

"How could you do such a thing, Patrick Michael Adams? How could you do such a thing to a fifteen-year-old child, your sister's best friend? How could you do this to us?"

"I don't know. I was so messed up then. I was not myself."

"You must have been the devil."

"Mrs. Adams," Timothy interrupted. "Patrick was very confused in his grief. His intimacy with Eve was wrong, but he was too full of grief and confusion at the time to recognize the gravity of his mistake. I don't believe the devil was present. Patrick is responsible for his mistake."

"Responsible? Are you ready to be responsibly married and working to raise this child? This child that you are responsible for?"

"Not now. I can't do that right now."

"Well, buddy, just as soon as you are old enough. You can say goodbye to sports in the meantime."

"Beth." His father finally opened his mouth.

"What?"

"We need to let this sink in. Don't make blanket statements."

"What? All this time, I was Eve's confidant. She told me there was no father. I trusted her and God, when really it was all just hormones and weakness."

"She didn't lie to you. It isn't about you," Patrick said. "She believed what you wanted her to believe. You lured her into your Bible stories that made her feel safe. She blocked it all out to protect herself, and you encouraged it by filling her head with God and the baby Jesus. She only remembered what happened when she went into labor. She was not trying to hurt *you*."

"And where did this happen—in my home? In your bed? Not in Grace's bed?"

He hung his head.

"There are no words!"

(PATRICK)

I felt a bubble in my belly that flowed up like vomit from deep inside and into my mouth and out.

"There are words," I shouted. "There are a lot of words! You. You and your perfect God made us go to the play when we had homework and it was storming outside. Grace had a biology test and you said it wasn't as important as the dumb Bible play! You had a migraine, but you wouldn't let me drive. You wouldn't get out of the window, and I couldn't get to Grace in the back seat. If you had listened to us and made us do our homework, and study for tests, Grace would be alive. If you had been like other mothers and believed in biology, Grace would have taken her test and graduated from high school and found love and gotten married and had babies. You. You did this and you are telling me that I am the devil. Nothing I have done, not drinking or drugs or sex or having a baby could be as bad as killing Grace. Tell your God that!"

I did not wait to hear what they had to say. My mother fell to the floor and wailed, a sound like an animal, and I slammed the door and went into the streets where I ran until I couldn't anymore.

(MRS. ADAMS)

I told the men to leave. Timothy and my husband. They were trying to be consoling, and I could not be consoled. When I could stand and breathe, I took the keys to the car and drove far out to where the road opens to the sky. I drove and talked to God where no one could see me ranting on and on. When I reached the old apple orchard where Grace and Patrick loved to pick pumpkins every October, I stopped and got out and bought a glass of juice from the stand. I took a walk down the rows of trees and remembered. Then I got in the car and drove to her grave. We buried Grace at the top of a hill under an oak tree at the prettiest cemetery, not the closest one. I knew it would be strong and protect her fragile little bones while they returned to the earth. I wanted her to see all around the beauty of the land. She was near another child who had been taken too young. When I went to be with her, I could spend hours looking around at the gentle hills and the sad people placing their flowers.

What Patrick said was horrible, of course. He has always been a gentle boy and the vulgar words and his ferocity and anger were like gunshots to me. He wanted to hurt me, and maybe I was waiting to be hurt. I have been waiting for someone to tell me it was my fault. No one ever did. Patrick finally had the courage. I will always love him. But I will not give up on God. My beliefs are as good as anyone's. At least God helps me. And if He does not help Patrick now, then I will wait until the day that He does. It will come.

I knew that Eve was sleeping in Gracie's bed. I was happy she was coming to us for comfort. I knew that Patrick wasn't sleeping, and I knew that he looked at her differently. I had such a strong feeling that Eve's baby was somehow connected to Grace. But still, I wanted God to be the connection. I wanted to let God do his work, and so maybe He did it in that way. Maybe I looked the other way so that Sparrow could come through them to heal us. God's hand, Gracie's blood, and Eve and Patrick all wrapped up in a new life. I could have stopped Eve from coming. I could have locked the window. I could have intervened and told her parents. Instead, I let it be, and now I am a grandmother. I lost my daughter and gained a granddaughter. Nevertheless, Patrick will be responsible. There, I will step in. He can hate me for a long time and blame me. He does not know how I blame myself. His hate does not come close to the hate I have for myself. When he was three and I would not let him watch TV, he said, "I hate you," and I put him in his room. I was wounded and went weeping to Frank. But Frank said it was normal for children to hate a parent for saying no. He was not even surprised. After that, Patrick always kept his feelings in. Grace was the one who told me everything.

Later that evening, Patrick came home.

"I am sorry for hurting you. I understand if you want me to move out."

"We do not want you to move anywhere. We want you to get help," I said. "We all need help. We will meet with Father

McInnis. Not Timothy. And we will plan our future as a family and we will ask for forgiveness, and we will bless this child and give her what she needs until you can support her. Patrick, you can make your own choice about God, but in this house, we are His children. In your house, you can make your own rules."

Patrick stayed in his room, mostly. He started studying more. He came home from school after practice. He called her every day. I could tell he was talking to her. After the band-aid was ripped off, leaving us raw, we slowly healed. We were easing into this new world. Though I had always balked at the idea, we went to see a psychologist as a family. For some reason in that room, we learned to say the things we really felt. There were some surprises all around. But I stood my ground about God. Yes, I believe Grace is in Heaven where I will see her again. And I also believe I am partly responsible for that accident. And many days I wish I could die, and on others, I want to live to see Sparrow grow up. Patrick seems finally relaxed now that he has said his truth. I feel like he can recover now.

CHAPTER 18

God

H e was ready. Now that he had told his parents, he was very calm. He had been still, thinking. And he was sleeping better. For the first time in over a year, he was not running and lifting every minute. He was laying on his bed, letting all the thoughts, ugly and horrible and new and scary, fly in and out. After the terrible conversation with his parents, he called me again. Sparrow was nine days old.

"I'm ready now," he said. "Can I come to see her?"

"Of course. My mom will be gone this afternoon. Do you want to come over then?"

"Yeah. As soon as I can."

She was asleep as usual. He recognized the bassinet.

"Your mom gave it to me."

"Oh yeah, I've seen it in pictures. I guess it was in the basement all this time."

He stood at my bedroom door.

"It's okay. She won't wake up."

He came in and tiptoed over until he could see her face. She was wrapped in her swaddle and her dark hair poked out. He stopped mid-room and took some breaths. His forehead wrinkled and he bit his cheek. Then he took a step forward as she sighed in her sleep. He sat on my bed next to the cradle. He reached out his hand and he placed his finger on her curled fingers, then her hair. He didn't look at me, or at the floor. He breathed slowly and bent over her. His lips parted and he turned to me.

"Wow. I thought she would be strange. I'm not a baby person. But she isn't. She's like a doll."

"I know."

He sat on the edge of my bed, and I picked her up and put her in his big arms. He held his breath and did not take his eyes off her as she stretched.

"Wow," he whispered. "If there is a God, I think this is it. Right here."

I looked at him, then at her. I breathed. I saw it, too. It was right there in the room. Maybe everyone thinks there is a God when their own baby is born. It is like seeing something for the first time that has been around forever. I don't know what I think of religion anymore, but my perfect baby . . . she is the proof there is more than any of us know.

CHAPTER 19

Mother

Six months later . . .

P atrick's hair is long again. The baby lost hers, and now she looks a little like me in baby pictures and a little like Grace too. Funny, we both had a kind of brown fuzz, and mine went one way, blonde and curly, and hers the opposite. So, I know that Sparrow is undecided. She could be anything, she's full of possibility.

We have been back in school for three months. It is almost Christmas again. So strange how it all turned out. People whispered, of course, and looked me up and down for about a week, and then there was football and yearbook and college applications, like anyone had time for my weirdo life. My mom was right; teenagers are just thinking about their own stuff. But Gaby was there for me, documenting teen mom life. She stayed my new best friend and helped me get through the transition back to school, and especially math every night. She had an amazing video of Sparrow's birth and was doing a project for her college applications. No one said anything mean directly to me. A few people said I looked great and, wow, they couldn't believe I am a mother.

Patrick and I speak in the halls now. We are actually friends. People never harass him about being a teen dad. Apparently, popular jocks just get high-fived for that kind of thing. He said his friends teased him about me because I was not his type, and stuff. They wanted to know how his parents hadn't killed him, but nothing more than that, although he was probably leaving a lot out for my sake. Addie is in my social studies class, and I feel like she looks at me funny, when she never would have even noticed me before. Patrick is back on the lacrosse team. The coach went to his parents and convinced them to let him play and take the scholarship offers that were coming. His dad stepped in and made it happen. He is expected to get good grades and visit the baby every other day too, so sometimes we do homework together. It is weird that he does this, and seems to like it, when I thought she would just be mine alone. He loves to play on the floor with Sparrow and feed her sometimes. My parents are very impressed with Patrick. They have assured him that they will support us financially until he and I can take over. My mother was the one who suggested that we should let his mother spend time with the baby.

"She has lost so much. Just imagine losing your only daughter. God can't make up for family." We tried to imagine.

Sometimes we go running together. He is different in the way you would be when you are now a father and everyone else is a child, and he seems to be somewhere else, not in high school. He is just looking forward, I think, planning the future. He told me he wants to go to medical school. There are boys more popular than he is now, and I think he is comfortable with that. He says he didn't like all the attention anyway.

My mother adores the baby, so she accepts her new life. I think she is glad to have a break from the volunteer world and she is surprised by this unexpected love. But I make sure she never has to babysit when I am not in school. And I know this is not the way it is for most teen moms, so we keep giving to Planned Parenthood and when asked, I always say I am so lucky because I have so much help, and everyone is there making sure we stay on the path to college and onward, and that Sparrow gets her needs met.

I am already thinking about what I am going to tell her about her unusual creation. I don't want her to think it was romantic or easy. Patrick did not want his mom to even see Sparrow, but after telling her to her face that she will not control him anymore, he set his own boundaries with her and relented. He brings her to their house one day a week while we are in school. Then I started going over on Fridays with her like old times. Mrs. Adams, of course, is beyond thrilled. She takes what she is given and does not ask me about God. So what if she sings in Sparrow's ear "Jesus Loves Me" and baptizes her in the sink when I am not looking. I think she finally sees that there is more than one way to love a child, or even believe. I hope that Mrs. Adams learned some things. And the way she treats Patrick now is proof. He is still her son, but she respects him. And my girl, she is so loved, and that's all that matters.

School is harder now that I am a junior and I have to take AP classes. But I am fortunate in that she is a really good baby. She naps for my mom and the babysitter who comes three days a week to relieve us. She goes to sleep at 7:00 at night and I am free to work. There are some bad nights, and I get frustrated and there are times I just want to be alone, for sure. My dad got me a jog stroller, so I am running a lot. One day last week Patrick and I ran all the way to the state park while Sparrow kicked her feet and squealed. I don't know what will happen to us. I am almost seventeen. He is graduating this year. We are a funny little family, and we will be forever linked. I figure he will find someone perfect for him in college, as he will start his life over in a new state with people who don't know what he has seen.

As for me, I was eating lunch in the cafeteria last week and Jake Lowe from orchestra sat down beside me. He and Gaby and I started talking about our English project. We are all in the same class. Last night he texted me to see if I wanted to work on it with him. I am going to his house on Sunday, and he said he would order pizza. I looked at myself in the mirror after I brushed my teeth, and for the first time, maybe ever, I saw someone curious: a girl with a sort of pretty face and cool hair.

The End

ACKNOWLEDGEMENTS

I would like to thank my friend, Joanne Holdridge, for reading my little novel all in one sitting on a computer screen and encouraging me to believe in it; Salome Perez, who told me that I never needed to try to publish my writing, but fear of failure was not a good enough reason; my daughter, Kalle, who was the first person to read *Eve* and give me solid pointers, even when she is not at all about pregnant teenage girls or God; Keaton, for all her creative and tech knowledge and encouragement; Jackson, for never complaining as I was forever banging at the keys throughout his childhood; Caroline Castro, for my beautiful cover; Kate Winter, who held my hand at the finish line; and finally my husband, Gary, who puts up with my loner, writerly ways when all he wants is an adventure for us to share.

ABOUT THE AUTHOR

Eve Immaculate is Robin Fox's first novel. She writes at her kitchen table with a splendid view of the oaks when she is not reading, walking dogs, helping her mother, holding NICU babies, pulling weeds or doing Pilates. She is the mother of three amazing people and lives with her husband, two dogs and a kitten in Miami, Florida.

CPSIA information can be obtained
at www.ICGtesting.com
Printed in the USA
BVHW041652250423
663034BV00018B/260